LITTLE ONES

LITTLE ONES

GREY WOLFE LAJOIE

HUB CITY PRESS
SPARTANBURG, SC

Book design: Kate McMullen
Cover image: Lou Benesh
Author photograph © Jane Morton

First printing
Printed in the U.S.A.

Library of Congress
Cataloging-in-Publication Data

Names: LaJoie, Grey Wolfe, 1991- author.
Title: Little ones / Grey Wolfe LaJoie.
Description: Spartanburg, SC : Hub City Press, 2024.
Identifiers: LCCN 2024012040 (print)
LCCN 2024012041 (ebook)
ISBN 9798885740395 (trade paperback)
ISBN 9798885740449 (epub)
Subjects: LCGFT: Short stories.
Classification: LCC PS3612.A49 L58 2024 (print)
LCC PS3612.A49 (ebook)
 DDC 813/.6--dc23/eng/20240422
LC record available at https://lccn.loc.gov/2024012040
LC ebook record available at https://lccn.loc.gov/2024012041

These stories appeared first appeared in the following journals: "The Locksmith" in the *Threepenny Review*, reprinted in *The 2023 O. Henry Prize anthology*, and in *The 2023 Pushcart Prize Anthology*; "work" in *Copper Nickel*; "Ampersand Jansen" in *Joyland*; "Maria" in *Yemassee*; "Interview with the Pope" in *Puerto del Sol*; "Saturday" in *Heavy Feather Review*; "Mention of Flesh" in *Mid-American Review*; "Snek & Goose" in *Meridian*; "Unfished, Unfinished" in *Shenandoah*; "Questions" in *Bat City Review*; "INTERVIEW WITH HORSIE" in *New Delta Review*; "How Come All the Schools Shutted Down" in *Cosmonauts Avenue*

HUB CITY PRESS
200 Ezell Street
Spartanburg, SC 29306
864.577.9349 | www.hubcity.org

CONTENTS

QUESTIONS

il

Name:
SSN:

QUESTIONS:

Please take your time in answering the following questions to the best of your ability.
Your responses are integral. Please use only a No. 2 pencil.

1. Before we go further, to what extent are you disappointed by the form presented here before you? Would you describe said disappointment as more acute or vague? Explain:

2. Describe something that could be achieved [in the remaining time] that might mitigate the disappointment:

3. Circle any of the following words which you feel best characterize the experience thus far:

Raw	Apathetic	Absurd
Relatable	Swol	Heartbreaking
Lyrical	Incriminating	Thicc
Punchy	Baleful	Rollicking
Hokey	Wack	Unputdownable
Sententious	Rhetorical	Hubristic
Slangy	Turgid	Savage
Refreshing	Sick	Mysterious
Elliptical	Withering	Ambitious
Luminous	Sagacious	Sexy
Didactic	Zany	Triumphant
Zealous	Flawed	Groundbreaking
Mean	Verbose	Fake
Shakespearean	Aggressive	Heuristic
Extra	Pointless	Woke
Celebratory	Histrionic	Noxious
Feckless	Lit	Serpentine
Therapeutic	Apologetic	Kooky

4. So, what's your sign?

5. Never mind about that. Of the following, which historical figure do you find most inspiring? Please choose only one:

- ○ Toulouse-Lautrec
- ○ George, of the Jungle
- ○ Henry Ford
- ○ Pope Victor the Terribler
- ○ Arian Grand
- ○ Humpty Dumpty
- ○ Diogenes the Cynic
- ○ Tinkerbell Hilton
- ○ Alan Iverson
- ○ Ulysses S. Grant
- ○ Tibetan Monks
- ○ Prefer not to say

6. Tell me a little about your dreams:

○ I was digging through rich red mud and uncovered the face of my mother. She was smiling but her eyes were tightly shut. This alarmed me. And then I felt nothing...

○ I had been sentenced to prison, though this was nothing out of the ordinary, soon enough I would be released. I could wander the prison freely, and I entered a cavernous stainless-steel restroom, wherein I tried to wash all my clothes in a toilet. took them off and shoved them down into the bowl. Then I flushed.

○ I was laying on a little rubber raft in the Atlantic Ocean. I found myself burn almost beyond recognition. This, I submitted to.

○ You were there! You were eating a salad but it was full of the most terrible insects. "Tell me a little about your dreams," you said.

○ Other.

7. Do you find this stimulating, this dance we're doing? Why or why not?

8. Where on this line of artistic imperatives do you feel I should attempt to fall?

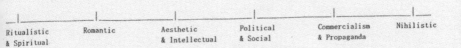

_|_____|_____|_____|_____|_____|___

Ritualistic   Romantic   Aesthetic   Political   Commercialism   Nihilistic
& Spiritual   & Intellectual   & Social   & Propaganda

9. In five to ten words, provide a caption for the following image [please do not cheat]:

_____

10. Now do so again, this time pretending you are your father:

_____

11. Why are you looking at me like that?

12. Let's continue. Please complete the following sentence:

"When I am alone, I am likely to _____."

○ sit in the darkness of myself
○ live like the light that kills
○ beware the stillness of the lord
○ mostly weeping

13. In the subsequent box, draw a pictorial representation of the moment you first grasped the concept of death:

14. Please list five things. Take as much time as you need:

- _____
- _____
- _____
- _____
- _____

5. Listen, maybe we got off on the wrong foot. Why don't we start over?

I understand you're very busy. Which of the following would be the best approach, moving forward, to keep from alienating you any further?

○ Ask me more about myself
○ Tell me a story
○ I'm still not speaking to you
○ Write some more sonnets, wussy
○ Stop please stop
○ Show yourself, coward!

Very well. I'll tell you a story:

Once, long ago, when the world was still ending, a very shy boxer stood gazing into the mirror. His eyes were quite small in his swollen face, and damp. *I was born at the end of the world,* he thought softly, watching himself blink. The life he led had wrought thick veins across his bald skull. Everyone he had known had borne witness to the slow explosion which consumed, incrementally, all things. When in those final years he would pass through the streets, the others appeared invariably angry to him. They were frustrated with the way things had come about. They could not understand. There was nothing to be understood, and this too was lost on them. He pulled himself away from his image and returned to the bag which, expertly, he punched. He was training to become the WBA Welterweight Champion while still such a thing existed. As he struck the bag, he envisioned a graveyard. In his mind's eye he flew very low over the graves, nearly touching them. At any given time it was night in his mind.

As the end begot itself it gave a horrid shudder and then hurled the world into frenetic waiting. This went on a long time. The boxer decided to go for a run. He was sore, but he did not think of this. He thought of what lay ahead. He let very little conflict with his forward movement, though on occasion he recalled his childhood dog, Noodle, and the strange sounds she had made when at last they'd had to put her down, and the knowing way she looked into his eyes that day.

The boxer ceased his running and sat down on the curb, among the hungry vehicles. *To lose something is so much,* he thought. Though already as it came the thought was leaving him again. He rose and continued forward.

3. Did you like the story?

      ○ Yes
      ○ No

THE LOCKSMITH

The locksmith cannot speak well. He never liked school. When he was a child, the others called him Tombstone. They threw things at him. Bottles and food waste and dirt clumps studded with gravel. Though he was much larger than them, he remained as still and as quiet as he could while enduring these acts.

The locksmith is not allowed a driver's license. He rides a bicycle from customer to customer, granting them entry. He likes to think about the number zero. He likes to think about time travel. He likes to think about shadows. He has watched many videos on each of these subjects.

When customers engage with him he is polite. The locksmith nods and goes about his work in silence. As a child he suffered a traumatic head injury at the hands of his step-father, and now he rarely smiles. It is painful to do so. The customers are deeply troubled by his presence, by his ineffable, clouded expression. But they must regain access to their homes, to their automobiles.

A woman calls the locksmith. She is screaming. Her son has shut himself inside her Lexus and refuses to open the door. Her only spare is with the father, she says, who is out of the country on business. Intermittently she shouts at her son while, it seems, banging on the hood of the car. She asks for an estimate and then gives the locksmith her address. The locksmith hangs up the phone and readies his equipment. Into a heavy black bag he packs his tension wrenches, his small key-cutting machine, his pick sets, a wedge, several blank keys. It is a large, three-story house on the far side of town and it takes him over an hour by bike.

When the locksmith arrives the woman is on her phone, pacing. She lowers the phone and covers the receiver. "Where were you?" she asks. "Liam might have died of dehydration waiting for you!" She wears dark, form-fitting jogging clothes and her gray hair is pulled up in a bun. The locksmith looks past her, toward the deep black car which glistens like fire. He steps toward the car and removes his bag. Inside the vehicle, a small blond boy watches him, motionless. The woman carries herself back and forth across the driveway speaking gravely into her phone. Sometimes she pauses to shout through the windshield at her son. "You little shit," she shouts. "You're going to have yourself a hell of a week after this you little shit." The boy does not acknowledge this. He continues to watch the locksmith, carefully. The two of them stare at each other through the glass. Something is being communicated. The locksmith leans down, shuffles through his black bag. The boy watches him in much the way a small animal would—a squirrel or a bird—if it were to find itself frozen in the locksmith's path. With terror the boy watches. From the heavy bag the locksmith removes a long, narrow tool. Abruptly the boy unlocks the car and runs toward his mother.

"Oh Liam," the woman says, hugging the boy. "Liam baby, are you okay?" She turns toward the locksmith. "You can leave now," she says.

࿊

In particular what the locksmith likes about shadows is that, although they occupy a three-dimensional area, we can see only a cross section of them. The cross section is a silhouette, a reverse projection of the object which blocks the light. But the shadow itself has a volume, dark and imperceptible.

It is still early in the morning, a cold sunny day in December, and the locksmith is riding to his next customer. The shape of his shadow stretches out before him. The customer he is visiting has dealt with the locksmith before. He is a man named Chuck, a realtor of some kind. Today Chuck is waiting on the steps of a property he has just purchased, a small bungalow with peeling white paint and shattered windows. He is smoking a cigarette and he waits for the locksmith to dismount his bike before speaking. "They told me this key worked on all the doors but it doesn't. I can't get into the basement." He hands the key to the locksmith and, although it serves no obvious purpose, the locksmith examines it carefully. SCHLAGE, the key reads. The locksmith breathes heavily.

He hands it back to Chuck and follows him into the house. The floor is littered with items of varying familiarity. Things bank up against the corners of each room, soiled beyond restoration. There are wrappers and shards, stray electrical wires, syringes, a phonebook ripped to pieces, an old tire. There are baby clothes and animal droppings and a heavily stained mattress. The smell is inscrutable.

Chuck leads the locksmith through the hallway, where every few feet someone has punched a hole into the drywall. Black mold wanders along in snaking bursts, digressing sometimes into these holes. The locksmith is careful not to step on a thing.

Chuck points to the basement door, then goes to the kitchen to inspect the gas lines.

The locksmith stands before the door. It is secured with two worn locks, and the work will take him some time to complete. He lowers his bag and begins.

The locksmith does not have friends. He has a pit bull terrier. When he found it, the dog was lying abandoned behind a shopping center. It was peppered with lacerations and unable to walk. He and the dog reside together in his deceased mother's house. Its coat is black but for the white streaks of fur atop its scars and the mist of gray under its eyes.

Each day when the locksmith comes home, the dog will hide under the bed for an hour or two, trembling. In the beginning, the locksmith tried to coax it out with food, but now he simply waits for these episodes to pass. By dark the dog climbs onto the bed and lies at the foot, watching the locksmith cautiously before drifting to sleep. In the mornings it eats, and only then allows itself to be touched by the locksmith. In this sense they coexist.

For two hours the locksmith works with patience and efficiency on the basement door. The first lock is a standard cylinder barrel and takes him very little time, but the second is rather elaborate, a paracentric keyway. He does not have the vocabulary to describe these things but he nevertheless understands them intimately and moves gracefully through the steps required to open them. Chuck has ordered a pepperoni pizza and offers it several times to him, but the locksmith cannot think of this. He must focus on his task. A lock is its own kind of language.

By noon he has fabricated a functioning key for each of the barrels. He duplicates them, puts them on a ring and brings them in to Chuck, who is crouched behind the oven. Chuck rises and takes the keys. His hands are dark with grease. From his wallet he removes three twenty-dollar bills and holds them out to the locksmith. "Pleasure," Chuck says. The locksmith takes the money and begins to leave.

"Hey," Chuck says, "don't you want to see what's down there?" The locksmith turns back to him, shakes his head and goes.

The symbol for zero is meant to encircle an absence, a nothingness. But the unbroken circle has come also to connote, paradoxically, everything. This excites the locksmith greatly. He has learned much about zero. He has learned that mathematicians and physicists are unsure whether zero is real, whether it should be treated as presence or absence. It is an interpretive problem. They are fiercely divided on the issue, he has learned. The answer determines a great deal: the nature of black holes and gravitational singularities and the origins of the Big Bang. The locksmith stays awake late into the night, watching videos on the subject.

He must ride across the river toward a small apartment building where an elevator has locked itself shut. Along the way the locksmith crosses a set of train tracks. On the tracks there is an animal, an opossum. She has been split in half precisely by the train. She is dead, certainly, though her stomach still bulges and writhes. The locksmith sets his bike aside, comes closer to the animal. From within her cleaved stomach there are newborn opossums, nosing their way out. Perhaps two dozen. They are pale pink and blind, moving haltingly into the hard winter light. Their flesh is so thin as to be translucent, the black eyes just visible beneath. The locksmith watches them squirm. He is unsure what to do. They are incredibly small. Each could fit with ease onto a tablespoon. After a time, he lowers his bag and begins to remove his tools. He takes out his tension wrenches and his key-cutting machine and his pick sets. He places them all neatly into a shrub, out of sight. He takes off his undershirt and lines the inside of his large black bag with it. Then, one at a time, he sets the opossums into the bag. In his hands they are crêpey and silken and periodically they seem to sneeze. The locksmith thinks to himself, *Hmm...*

The dog is bewildered by the locksmith's return so early in the day. For a time it stares at him, forgetting to hide. The locksmith finds an old cookie tin in the kitchen. His home is as it was when he inherited it. He takes the tin and lines it with socks. He places the opossums into the tin along with a jar lid filled with warm water. Into another lid he spoons applesauce. The dog watches curiously as he works. It sniffs at the air between them. When the locksmith glances at the dog it turns and leaves abruptly, disappearing into the bedroom for the rest of the night. Nervously, the locksmith looks into the tin. The small animals stumble vaguely into one another and then rest. He sets them on the kitchen counter, beneath a small reading lamp which he hopes will keep them warm. For the remainder of the day he sits and watches them.

In the morning the locksmith goes and retrieves his tools. They are coated in a thin layer of dew and he wipes them down carefully with a rag before placing them back into his bag. The woman who owns the apartment building with the locked elevator is not terribly upset about the delay. The name she gives is Ms. Alice. "People can use the stairs," she says, when he arrives. She speaks with an enigmatic European accent and wears heavy, riotous jewelry. The locksmith follows her up to the fourth floor, where the elevator was last opened. On the way she hums to herself an unrecognizable tune. Her voice leaps about the staircase. The locksmith walks closely behind, blushing at the sound.

It has been a long time since the locksmith has worked an elevator but he has not forgotten. First he must use a universal drop key to open the landing doors. Once inside he can determine the underlying issue.

"You know the great Houdini?" Ms. Alice asks him. The locksmith is kneeling before the elevator control panel, the woman standing behind him. He looks back at her, somewhat distressed. "He started as a locksmith," she says. "At the age of eleven he began as an apprentice for the local locksmith and soon he could pick anything open." The locksmith smiles painfully, nods and turns back to his work. "Have you seen his gaze?" she asks. "I think he had the most magical gaze. So terribly terribly morbid his gaze was." The locksmith is trying to focus. He has the key in the chamber but he must turn it just so in order to trigger the doors. Ms. Alice watches with her hand on her chest. "He was Hungarian you know. A lot of people don't know that. Hungarian and Jewish. They buried him alive but he clawed his way out. That was one of his tricks but he started panicking while he was digging up." Her jewels clatter carelessly as she speaks. "Later he wrote in his diary, 'the weight of the earth is killing.' That's what he wrote. Can you believe that? They had to pull his body up out of the dirt." The mechanism catches and the locksmith steps back. He takes his heavy pry bar and carefully works the doors open. "How lovely!" Ms. Alice says.

The elevator cab is stalled between floors and the locksmith has to crouch and step down into it. It is dim in the cab. The only light comes from the floor above, where Ms. Alice's feet are still visible, rising up from red shoes. The locksmith inspects the service key mechanism. It is a very simple tubular pin tumbler lock. It will take only a little while. Ms. Alice calls down into the shaft. "Are you thirsty?" she asks. "Would you like something to drink?" The locksmith mumbles something quickly. "What?" Ms. Alice says. He repeats himself carefully, his shoulders tense. There is a long silence and then the locksmith returns to his work, impressioning the lock with a blank. "Oh how I wish I could have seen him perform," Ms. Alice says. "Such a handsome, eerie man. Full of miracles. Full of wonder. Keep up your enthusiasm! He always said that! But then of course his final words were something altogether different."

In very little time the locksmith has restarted the elevator's operation. The lights flicker on at once and the doors close and of its own accord the cab begins to lift him. It rises eight stories and then opens up to the roof. Before him, the gray sky unfolds slowly, its cold light flooding the cab. A dark bird drifts down on the wind and lands just ahead of him.

Since he was a very small child the locksmith has thought of time travel. There is one theory he has learned which accepts the flow of time as a cognitive construct. This is the locksmith's favorite. According to this theory, were the locksmith to return to his past—such as the last time he saw his mother—he would have no experience of any temporal discontinuity. He would simply look backward in memory, reconstructing his childhood, or forward in expectation, guessing at the future. Were the locksmith to travel back through time, in other words, everything would feel as it does now. The locksmith thinks of this often. He thinks, who is to say I haven't just time-traveled? Who is to say time ever moves forward? Wordlessly he thinks these things to himself.

The locksmith waits for the elevator doors to close, then presses the button to go back down. When he returns Ms. Alice is there smiling. "That was quite the escape!" she says.

WORK

we move into a double wide   set out over the river   jules
looks after the baby and i go to the funerals   the doves have
to come back each and every one if even one dove is lost than i cant
break even and cant replace it   you have to think about
all the weeks of traning. the food i feed them. all the expenses
right out of the gate. the tagging   the registering   i dont
do this just for God after all i do this for jules and for the baby.
i tell myself exactly that each morning.   i remind myself
    you are doing this for jules and the baby

the other day at maude hewitts funeral a owl i mean a very large
owl was siting in a oak stairing and i mean stairing at my little
birds   just waiting for me to let them out owls being a natural
predator to the dove of course   so i refused to release and the
family   the hewitts   began to scream into my face
well   that did not exactly convinse me   yelling at me right
infront of all those unhappy morners   some people have no
control whatever   the doves looking up at me wondering what it
was all about   that noise   i did what i thought i had to do
for my livelyhood i put them up in the truck and drove off   let
me be clear i do not wish to be a crual man i do not wish to take
from no one but i have seen what a owl or a hawk can do to a
dove in mid air and it is not   a pretty sight   if those people
had got to see such a sight   it would do them   no spritual
favor   charles said im not sure i can give you another
buriel you can not keep acting this way these people are sensative.
sensative   to what i wonder? to who? you handed your grief over
to some stranger,   i want to say

23

i want to say   they took your beloved and washed her
body which a long time ago you would have washed   yourself
    they took her body and put spiked contact lenses over her eyes
to hold the lids shut forever   and glued her mouth up
and filled her with formaldihide   to make her look less dead
    you people   i want to say   you people think *i'm*
taking something   you already gave it   away
but i dont say none of that   i just get in my truck and close
the door   being   careful   not to slam it   and i drive away

SNEK & GOOSE

nek the snake and Goose the goose were in the parlor, pray-ing. Snek looked up from his prayer.

"Goose?" he said.

"Huh?"

"I was wondering about how come all the leaves had fell down."

"It's fall," Goose said.

"Yeah and they fell down and now it's all yellow and I can slide through it and all sneaky like!"

"Yes..." Goose replied.

Snek began to weave a tight circle around himself. "Sneky snek!" he said. "Sneky snek sneky snek sneky snek!"

"Snek, it's time to go to bed."

"But I have the bad feeling..."

"You say that every night."

"I do I do! I have the bad feeling!"

"Well just go to bed and let the dreams come in. It'll all come out in the wash."

"Can't you read me a story?"

"Not tonight Snek," Goose said. But Snek began to cry and howl until Goose conceded.

"Very well, but you first must wash your face and lie down in your sock. You must lie very still and close your eyes! Only then I will tell you a story."

"Story! Story! Story!" Snek said.

"Do as you're told..." Goose said.

"Story..."

Goose gave Snek the look and Snek did as he was told.

"Alright," Goose said. He lifted a very large picture book up and began to read. "Once upon a time there was a tall human boy named Grey. He had long, gray-green fingers and perfect rotting teeth. Everywhere he went fear lingered..."

Snek grew very excited and slithered up under his sock.

"One day, Grey was walking through the human world, hammering out the houses. His brother Retti stood beside him, cursing up a storm. 'This is a fucking nightmare,' his brother said toward the broad blonde human world. Retti had been the one who taught Grey how to hammer out houses, and now the two of them did this together, hammering from house to house. In the house where they hammered this day, Grey found a bird. The bird was named Thomas, though Grey could not have known this, for humans had long since lost their second sight, and could not any longer believe. The bird sat atop the kitchen faucet, pondering the cold linoleum castle humankind had wrought. At this visitation, Grey became ecstatic. 'Retti!' he called out. 'Retti! Retti!' He ran up the stairs to where the chop saw sat. Studs and joists strayed all overhead. Retti was there, leaning out of a window and smoking thoughtfully. Retti had been to prison several times, and it was those long years he thought of now."

"What's *prison*?" Snek asked suddenly.

Goose pondered this a moment. "Prison," he began, "is the place where humans put each other when they're not wanted."

Then he added, "It's administered through something they call *time*."

Snek looked down pensively at his tail, which lolled slightly from the edge of the bed. "Oh," he said.

Goose continued. "Sometimes Grey wondered about this place where his brother had spent so much time. They did not speak of it overmuch, though from time to time they drank elixirs. Only then did Retti disclose the darknesses he'd seen. Once, in the prison cafeteria, Retti watched his very good friend Dee endure something truly horrible at the hands of another human and, after this, Retti could not speak much with Dee, for the words came out of his brain all scrambled and sad."

"Elixir?" Snek asked.

"It allows them back into their animal impulses."

Snek thought about these words a while, but could make no sense of them.

Goose went on. "Grey spoke up eagerly. 'Retti! Retti!' he said. 'There's a bird in the house!' But Retti did not rise from the sill. He was deep in a cloud of thought, watching the trees sway. Just then, someone came knocking on the unfinished door. Grey went back down to the kitchen, to check on the bird. It had gone. The person who knocked on the door was their sister Sandra. They did not know how Sandra found out where they were working. They maintained not much contact with her, and her appearance in truth somewhat frightened them. She gazed at them eagerly. 'Can you cut this board for me,' she asked. Retti spoke politely to her and Grey watched. Sandra had schizophrenia and six B.A.s. She worked at the Salvation Army. Sometimes she spoke of the computer chip which had been placed in her molar, and the way it whined each time she passed a phone poll. Their father had done a number on Sandra. He had done a *number* on several of them, as a matter of fact. He had done a number on Sandra and he had done a number on Cathy and he had done a number on Dawn and he had done a number on Emerson and he had done a number on Retti and he had done a number on Jessie. Relative to them, Grey had been spared somewhat. This put the number at 9 at least, counting wives. Their father had hammered out houses too, before drinking himself away with elixirs. Before his death he had informed them each that the world was held together with nails. Grey hoped never to do a number on anyone."

"Ahhh!" Snek said. He had fallen asleep and awoken suddenly.

"Snek! It's okay Snek, you were just having a bad dream. It's okay."

"I dreamed there was a bright blue fox and it ated us up!"

"There there Snek. Everyone's fine. Everyone's fine." Snek trembled lightly in his sock and gazed at Goose in panic.

Goose decided to continue reading, to calm Snek down. "The house they hammered at was awfully rotten. This is why they had been hired to hammer it. Humans did not much care for rot, which they feebly sought to undo. They wanted only glistening signs of human poise.

"The board the brothers cut was for their sister Sandra's window-unit. It was meant to function as a side-panel, to keep all the heat far away. Sandra moved about the rotting house with ease. She spoke of the government and of an international cabal and of a new world order. She spoke of her own thoughts being broadcast on the radio, and of those persons that wished to do her in. She moved about the house emitting sharp, harried laughter, and spitting sometimes on the floor. A great deal of damage moved through her, like the water that rushes from fountain to air, spraying out in all directions. This, it seemed, was the way that damage always moved. Grey was tasked with measuring and cutting the board, while Retti spoke to the sister. 'I tried to call you,' she kept saying, spitting down onto the floor. 'I called over and over.' The skillsaw howled in Grey's hand. 'Oh, did you?' Retti said."

"What's *window-unit?*" Snek asked. He had curled up into a tight ball and from time to time he licked cautiously at the air.

"Window-unit is what the humans use to freeze the wind, to keep their covered flesh from sweating."

"Oh..." Snek said, with some amount of terror still residing in his voice.

"Sometimes Grey worried that it was not only Sandra, that this way of thought perhaps ran in the family. He wondered sometimes if there was evidence of it sprinkled through his art, lying there dormant and waiting. He felt often gutted, without center. He cut the boards precisely, and gave them to his sister, whom he found himself fearing. After Sandra left, Retti decided it was time to procure the day's elixirs, so he sent Grey to fetch some from the A.B.C. Store. Grey took the truck and drove along the mountainside. He very much liked to drive. It gave him the sense that he was free. It was an old red truck, and he had restored the poor engine himself. It did not run well but it ran. He allowed the machine to grumble through the human world in savage circular patterns, pretending for a moment he was wild. Then he came to the A.B.C. Store, where he bought twenty-three miniature bottles of Evan Williams elixir—for Retti did not wish to acknowledge the need for a pint—and drove back to the human house they were hammering. They referred to these as baby-bottles, and the empties littered the floor of their rusted out vehicle."

Snek was snoring softly, a bubble of snot building up at his nostril. Goose lay down the book and turned out the light. "Good night little Snek," he said. He wandered through the house for a time, ensuring all the lights were off. Then he went onto the porch to watch the moon. It crept up the night's sky at the most peculiar angle, and hung there as though stuck. I would never want to be human, Goose thought. I'm so glad to be a goose.

AMPERSAND JANSEN

Ampersand Jansen

Ampersand Jansen was riding his horse through the pines. "Hit don't bover me nun," he said, "the way the winds lash at the leaves. I'd as soon let a breeze hurt me dead than to set in the silence of hollows and wait." It was dark and it was night and the wind foretold such a violent rain, though Ampersand seemed merry. He bounced on the back of his roan. This was something altogether unpleasant to the horse, this bouncing, and any old day now she would decide to kick sad Ampersand dead. "Hat," he said, for this was the name he had chosen to give to the horse. "Hat I don't bleave I ever seent a sky such a color as this night's here. Makes my mind to wander it does." He turned his head and spit adroitly. "Hat," he said. "Hat! What color you reckon you'd call that sky there tonight? Roset? Carnelian? Oxblood?"

Hat thought softly to herself;
Caput mortuum, is what she thought.
Ampersand cogitated on the sky some
more, then chewed at a wad of his
long pale lover Aydelflæd's hair—
such soft and winding hair which
tasted of fennel and rue. He wished to
be united with her, for just some little
longer while. "Hit jess don't strike me
as the right shade to-night."

Ampersand and Hat rode tireless
through the dark, assuming that,
by morning, their small lives would
be once more illumined. Yet they
bounced along in a most foolish
direction; for in yonder's cabin lived
the maiden fair, and yonder's way
led likewise into coal-black sea, and
yonder's valley was the place where
hunger dwelt and where no life could
gather, and everything that stayed
beyond belonged as well to yonder.

But by and by they rode. Along the
ride the horse envisioned a mighty
black dagger of hounds at her feet,
barking and snapping most murderously. The horse had to keep up a
steady pace, so to keep from becoming
a meal. "Hit don't matter nun what I
got in my body," said Ampersand to

himself. "For so soon it all doth purge away into a bliss." He was speaking of the tumors, of the dozens of trembling tumors that wound their way through his poor pale body and caused the Great Pain. He spoke of the tumors in a silken manner, as though he had accepted what they whispered toward. But this, like so much of Ampersand's nature, was a show he put on for himself to watch.

And inside the horse's heart, something else: deep in the loamy red, a spire had begun to form. It was only now the size of a straight pin, a minor stalagmite in the organ's soft floor. For now Hat felt it as no more than a dull ache. But it would grow larger, much larger, would work its way as best it could toward the inky sky, and would thereon inscribe a wondrous message.

It was morning. Ampersand Jansen sat by the fire, eating him a egg wrapped in ham. Things were gentle inside, had not yet begun their more tremorous ache. Beside him Hat stood still asleep. In her dreams, magnificent flowers falling down from the sky, swallowing everything. Ampersand had removed his shirt and was sunning himself. The flies buzzed about his feet.

"Aydelflæd," he said. "*Aydelflæd, Aydelflæd, Aydelflæd!*" But this was just a name. By now he had little more to grasp than that, a small good air which came and went. He could not even remember the maiden's surname, or her favorite flavor of soap. He believed one perhaps began with an L. "O how eager time doth wrap its garrote round the soul," he blubbered. "How steady the piani wires tighten round the mind. How so! How so!" The horse was woken by these consternated yowlings. "Hat!" Ampersand said, overjoyed. "Hat you're back! I feel a sudden compression of the laffter fits awellin inside me I do." Hat was terribly annoyed. She thought of the cool cool icicles which hung from the trees where she was born. The glassy blades dropped down through her mind, pierced the soft snow below.

"Hat," said Ampersand. "I bleave we oughta go off an take us a dip in the wuter. Or we could venture up into the peaks." He removed his socks from a tree branch and pulled them up over his gnarled yellow feet. "I'm a mighty restless fella this mornin. In truth I don't spose I know which way I'd rather wander." As he spoke to the horse, he thought to himself, *Aydelflæd Aydelflæd Aydelflæd.* This, a song which lost more meaning the more that it was sung.

Hat watched him lace up his boots. She was not certain that Aydelflæd even existed. In all the years they'd been together, she had not once seen a woman even glance at Ampersand's old dirty tooch of a person. In truth, Hat suspected all this was no more than a poem he told to himself. It was sad, really. She pitied the man. Soon he would be an old churl drooling on his deathbed, still trying to tell funny stories to account for what was lost.

Ampersand removed his jug of wyne from out his pouch and began to guzzle. The stuff was sweet and stale against his lips, and driveled down his beard. He was never without it.

Inside the horse's heart the spire grew marvelous and heavy. It glistened by an unknown light. It weighed as much as bronze and sprouted through the horse's throat. Soon it would make its way into the world and ascend.

"I don't like you," Ampersand said to his face, which the water's surface was reflecting back at him. "You're makin me look bad."

They rode a long while and then came to a church. Ampersand tied Hat up to a post and went in. Inside the church was flooded with hellebore. Wild white blooms hung from every corner of the space. Hellebores flooded the aisles. They flooded the chancel and flooded the nave and flooded the crossing and flooded each apse. In the foyer they fell to the floor, and across the transept too. Ampersand looked to the ceiling, to the heavenly dome. Flooded.

A humpbacked priest stood at the alter installing more flowers. "Monsignor!" Ampersand said to a priest. "Monsignor I need to do me a confession!" He trundled his way toward the pulpit. "I long to be shrived!" He stopped trundling at the foot of the alter and looked up at the brittle old man. "You busy?"

The priest gazed down at him and

sighed. "My child," he said, "a service is to begin fifteen minutes from now—A funeral." He took a hand-kerchief from his pocket and blew away a sniffle. "Might you," he asked, "not wait until after?"

"Glad to!" Ampersand said. He stepped back a ways and sauntered through the quire, his boots parting the perfectly placed bouquets. At a far back pew he took a seat and bowed his head.

Aydelflæd, he prayed. *Aydelflæd Aydelflæd. Please Lord, Aydelflæd.* Then the congregation began materializing, and took their seats around him.

Hat was tied up outside. She had a song stuck in her head. It went *Doom dah dah dah, doom doom, Dah doo doom doom doom, dah dee dee dah diddle, dee dah, doom diddle doom. Doom. dah dee, dah, doom, doom doom doom. Dah dee, dah dee dee. Didle dee dah doom doom.* But she could not recall the title. A very small child approached her.

"Hello mister horsie!" the child said. "Want a candy?" Brusquely he fed a fat chocolate bar to Hat, which she appreciated greatly, having had not much more than the corn residue Ampersand fed to her all these long years. A wild thrill moved through her and she gave an involuntary whinny. The child giggled. "Want another?" he asked, revealing a chocolate bar just like the last. Hat whinnied again, her legs trembling with pleasure. She felt just like a pony, like something from that wild far off world. The child lifted the candy up toward her. Then, somewhat suddenly, the spire surfaced. It emerged from between Hat's lips, pierced the candy with its finial, and went swiftly on its way. The boy fell to the ground and watched the spire lift like smoke toward the sky. Hat watched too, her head thrown back, for there was little more that she could do. The spire had grown beyond her capacity. Rapidly it rose into the trees overhead, knocking loose the leaves. The spire was tapered and, while the diameter at its tip was no more than that of a rolling pin, its base's width was yet to be revealed. Still, Hat felt no discomfort as it rose out of her. Though nor did she feel any particular joy. The spire continued to rise higher, taking the small chocolate bar up with it and casting its shadow across the land. As she watched the thing ascend she thought, *Nottamun Town*. For that was the song she had had in her head.

Ampersand was weeping fiercely. The priest had delivered the most moving of speeches about that young lady, that fine young lady whose name he had not caught, and now he was blowing his nose in his sleeve.

"Such fine songs you sang up from the darkness of this life," he said to the priest. "Such fine and lonesome things wrung out from the rag of misry. Monsignor I bleave I heard the very footsteps of the lord in yer speech."

"Very good my child," said the priest. "Very good. Now what do you wish to confess?" Ampersand looked toward the confessional. "Oh," said the priest, "The shroud will not be needed, for I have seen already the light play off your visage." This troubled Ampersand, though he knew not why.

"Well sir..." Ampersand began, but he could not quite articulate his sins succinctly. He began again. "I... I was..."

But then the deacon rushed in.

"Father!" he said. "Father! The Devil is come down unto us!"

Ampersand's dreams had been awful for years. In each of them, the ground collapsed. The trees stayed in place, but the earth around them crumbled away, and he and all the animals plummeted endlessly. He would clutch at the roots of the trees, but they moved like serpents away from him, allowing him to fall. He had had such a dream just last night, and woke with a terrible start.

By now a sizeable crowd had formed around Hat, who strained bravely under the weight of the spire. The child who had fed the horse the chocolate bar was being questioned now. Though often those that questioned him became distracted by some new stride the spire made. Already it had pierced the clouds.

Ampersand Jansen was not altogether surprised to find his horse in such a state as this. He had often suspected that there was something grand about her, something terribly grand, though he could never say what.

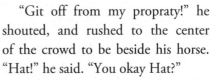

"Git off from my propraty!" he shouted, and rushed to the center of the crowd to be beside his horse. "Hat!" he said. "You okay Hat?"

It was true he had not loved her as best as he could have. All over the world there are men guilty of this, and he was one. Still, a feeling began to work its way through him and there was no name for it he yet could find that fit as well as *love*. "Oh Hat," he said. "Dear sweet lovin Hat. The best old roan alive."

The horse watched the spire grow. It welled out of her like a song. Soon it would break her jaw, crush her weary torso and topple itself, sending debris throughout the small village. For now it went on rising, the people watching patiently.

"To thee do we cry," the Deacon muttered softly. "To thee do we send up our sighs, our mourning and our weeping in this vale. Turn then thine eyes of mercy toward us, and after this our exile, show unto us the blessèd fruit..."

45

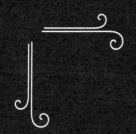

IDLY

At the Super Center, Crutchfield has blood in his stool. He comes to me sometimes for advice, so I know.

"Can I get fourteen ounces of the Bluefin?" Crutchfield says.

"Blood is the universal symbol of stress," I advise. Crutchfield furrows his brow, stares into the glass counter between us, all the gleaming gills. Very pensive. He waits for me to put on my stretchy gloves. I can see there is stress, but to tell Crutchfield more than once would counter-produce. In my hand, the fish is frozen in a gasp.

"There's nothing really to worry about," I tell him.

Behind Crutchfield are all the angry hordes, smashing pickle jars, flipping cheese samples. All over town, there are these angry hordes. I can't understand them. The hordes are angry today because all of the libraries are closing or something. Chaos is looming. The burning reflection of looming chaos flickers off my glass counter as we chat, illuminates Crutchfield's face with some funny sanguine color, and glows in the blacks of the black fish eyes. The hordes are beyond help, but there is still Crutchfield.

He tells me how difficult it can be to love, and I hand him the fish.

"Have you ever been in love?" he asks me. I keep one hand behind my back, fingers opening and closing. Opening and closing. The latex gives a yelp.

"Once," I say. But really, I hope he doesn't press the subject further.

"At first, it scared me," Crutchfield says, "Deep dark red in the pit of the bowl. The water, pink throughout." Crutchfield has this way of talking, loose wrist waving around his words, long hesitant pauses. Eyes on the gills. "Now though, I'm pretty used to it. It's been three weeks like that." He takes a breath and looks up at me. I have to peel my shirt from the dampness on my chest. Corporate won't let us run the AC. Heat's been bad this summer, dog days all the way through. I tilt my head forward, gaze over the rim of my glasses at Crutchfield, so I can look him in the eyes without seeing too much. I guess I should say something kind to him, wise, but what comes out instead's the price.

Our Super Center is the last of its kind. A lone oak, jointed lines ribbed out toward dismay. A vanishing corporate cloud, made up of the careful steady drip, our heartbeats. Since he quit last fall, Crutchfield has worked in a wine store. But he used to work right next to me, in Meat.

Once, just before he left, out back we found a box of blind kittens. They couldn't open their eyes and they stumbled around in the sun. I wanted to give them away, but Crutchfield convinced me to carry them back to my house. Matted orange fur and cardboard. They wouldn't let the things onto the bus so I carried them. Crutchfield lit a cigarette and walked with me and we talked. His voice reminds me of my mother's voice, thick and easy coming out. I remember, it was fall then, and the sun was orange and the leaves were orange and the ground was covered orange. It was nice.

Rest of the day the other sellers offer samples, coupon machines froth and churn, customers curse each other, the hordes at it with their inferno of change. I just think about Crutchfield. The way he simmers sometimes, like a movie. Sweet wet eyes. How his mustache trembles when he speaks, the trick he does with the cigarette smoke. The way his comb over writhes in the wind. His sorry smile. I love him all.

"Five dollars a pound!" scream the others, "Five dollars a pound!" but I can't. Too much ennui about myself. I know I'm not alone. Others around here have started also to feel some ennui about themselves. Crutchfield, for example. I imagine he stands in his yard these days, rips the cord back with all his wilted strength. Crutchfield is sick. Some kind of heavy cloud of doubt in his stomach. Sky filled with gray, shadows like bruises over his lush lawn. There are certain things that don't work anymore, and one of them is his lawnmower. Ripping the cord, but no rumble to speak of.

There is some disturbance over in Housewares. A woman, shouting. Her hair wild with sweat, a heavy gasping shriek. She shouts at her husband and he paces a small circle. Underneath my kiosk I have a small bottle of bourbon. Now is when I take a nip. The guy keeps pacing and sometimes he kicks this metal trash can and it gives this rumble. Everyone is staring by now. The girl is just talking. We don't know what she's saying. She's doing little hops. Guy punches the trashcan again, big rumble, glances at his hand. Punches again with the hand. There's a line of elderly men viewing. Some of them are drinking coffee from little styrofoam cups. I wonder sometimes about this town, with the hordes and all. The woman says I wish you wouldn't get so angry. The man says everyone in this town gets angry. His face is a little heavy with meat and age and I can see two veins in his forehead. She has her fist up, trembling. She says only the garbage men, only the dropouts get so angry. All this is great, but I'm thinking about Crutchfield. Poor Crutchfield.

Everyone keeps on staring at the couple, but now an older woman has arrived and the man just breathes heavily and glances at his hand while the girl cries into her mother. Nothing else happens but we wait.

After work I walk because the buses don't run anymore. On the way I see a man with a brick in his hand, chanting, "Bigger cages! Longer chains!"

I smile at him and he hisses. It's a long walk home and my feet hurt, but my heart hurts too. "We are the crisis!" he shouts, "We are the crisis!" but I already know.

At home I lie in bed. I take off my eyeglasses and I lie in the shadows. Without my glasses everything is softer. My eyes go limp and I listen to the hordes. Shouts like thunder. When I close my eyes, all I can picture is fish. Rows of silver scales. They are chanting something outside my window. What it is I don't care. When will they stop? Where is their ennui?

As I close my eyes I picture the man from earlier, punching the trash can and staring at his fist. But I can't remember his face, so I see Crutchfield. It's hard to think about. I know Crutchfield is ill, and he knows he is ill, irreparably ill. But we go on like this. There are certain things that are not expressed easily. For Crutchfield, I can speak only through my fish. The snapper for his eyes. A marlin for his fears. Half pound of tuna for the bugs at his feet. Like the coy poet, I show him each lean silver Dory and in this way I shout I love yous. Flipping little mackerels and in this way I say it hurts.

On top of all of this, I am trying to quit smoking. I lie awake most of the night writhing in the heat. Sometimes I go out on the porch to tremble. For sleep, I wear three Nicorette patches. I sit at the edge of my bed and try to arrange the little beige squares for optimal nicotine intake. Some of the shapes I evaluate for effectiveness: V shape, triangle, pyramid, row of diamonds, row of squares. No matter what, I can hardly taste it. I begin to rearrange the furniture.

Jib wakes me up with his coarse licks. I open my eyes and his little rusty face stares up at me. Jib is one of my orange cats. They aren't blind anymore, but they still have problems. Jib has scoliosis. Bish has a tremor. Walter is missing his frontal lobe, so he kills all the flies and gathers them by the door. Meredith bleeds.

Jib leaps from my lap, onto the floor. His spine is a frozen wrinkle, and his back zigs into his neck with each stride. I follow his broken steps into the kitchen. In there, the phone is ringing and Meredith is bleeding on the microwave. A spider lives in the pile of dirty dishes and I can't find my glasses. The phone's ringing is a vibrant black, a thickening ambient welt in my head. I open the fridge and pull out the expired hummus and Kool Aid. The phone is still ringing. Outside the hordes are just beginning to blossom into the lungs of the day. Maybe it's Crutchfield calling. I pick up the phone.

"Hello? Hello?" I say. But he has hung up just before I answered. Does the pain ever go away? I want to say. I want to say, the sadness of you breaks my heart. I hang up the phone.

Last week Crutchfield arrived at my stand with a young man by his side. Hair short and blond. I did not like him. Giggles and a sneeze. No ennui at all. He watched me the whole time, waiting for me to give him yet one more excuse to laugh. His hand resting idly on Crutchfield's shoulder, dainty and ringless, whispering questions into his ear. I do not like him. I was glad when it started to rain. The way he panicked through the parking lot. His blond hair turned heavy and dark. I took a nip of the bourbon then.

Crutchfield says the saddest things sometimes. Just before he left, as the rain picked up, he waved his cigarette at me and told me what nice eyes I had.

BABY

ometimes, with these wires, the electricity can leap through the air. You'll be busy working, holding the frayed end of a wire in your left hand, very focused, very professional, while down on the ground another, unrelated wire that you've cut earlier is lying in wait, lying like a snake among the darkened wisps of insulation. What happens is, the electricity wants to go—it wants to keep moving, moving, always moving onward anyway it can, and when it gets a whiff of the other wire, some feet away, it leaps through the air to reach it. They call it 'arcing,' and it is scary as shit. Anyway, this had happened twice that morning as I was demonstrating all my tricks to Baby—the electric arc vaulting up from the ground and into the wire I held like some drunk witching trick. I began to suspect I was giving Baby the wrong impression, because each time this occurred he would laugh deep into his belly, and even clap. But after a couple of hours I had gotten everything wired up so that nothing caught fire and the overhead fan it fed still spun like it was supposed to. Then, I told Baby to try it himself.

The first thing to know about Baby was that he didn't do the things he used to do. He didn't even laugh the way he used to—his famous laugh. When people spoke he used to watch them like a predator, waiting. Then, without any warning, and for reasons no one ever understood, he would pitch his monstrous body back and howl relentlessly. No one who ever witnessed this spectacle did so without flinching. It was the first light of his terror, a glimpse of something bottomless.

Baby didn't do those things now, it was true, but you could still see something from before behind his eyes—if you knew him well enough you could—something feral and unfeeling but now unable to come forth. He didn't wish to speak of it, or claimed he didn't remember, but the problem was he'd suffered a very bad blow to the head one night, about a year ago, while he was shaking down some helpless dupe. He didn't know the kid's brother was around the corner with a fire-poker, waiting. Baby avoided charges but he had to sit in the hospital for so long that people started to assume he'd died. Now that he was out, we feared him more than ever. It hadn't made him stupid or anything, the head injury. But everyone could see that certain lights had been turned off, and others were switched on now. Anyway, out of pity or fear or something they'd gotten him this job with Robbie and I, helping this old man remodel his house out in the country. The old man said he'd done this kind of work before, but it was clear early on that none of us had any clue what we were doing.

"If that jolt gets you," I said to Baby, "I'm pretty sure it'll kill you or paralyze you or something," and I went downstairs.

There were studs in short stumps hanging down from the ceiling, their cut edges random and jagged, threatening. The old man gazed at me like he always did, surprised and searching as a child.

"Do you think this is enough space?" Robbie asked. He was wielding the reciprocating saw I'd seen him acquire just last month, in exchange for a bass guitar that wasn't his to pawn.

"Enough space for what?" I asked.

"For the gallery!" Robbie said, as though this should make it all obvious. Robbie set down his saw and picked a tape measure up out of the rubble.

Out of all of us, Robbie knew the most. He was the one who had convinced the old man in the first place to hire us. He had known just enough to keep the charade going. We had been at it already almost six months by then—Robbie giving everybody orders, conferring with the old man every so often about what he wanted us to do, and then explaining to him why it wasn't possible. By the time Baby came onto the job the house was totally exploded—two exterior walls had been knocked down, and certain rooms you had to know not to walk through, because the floor had been ripped out, and if you forgot you'd fall back through to the first story.

The old man and I watched as Robbie went around the newly hollowed out space taking measurements of things and writing them down onto a scrap of cardboard.

"Susan had always wanted children," the old man said. "And I didn't." I hoped he was only talking to some sort of hallucination, but then he turned to me. "I didn't want children, but I was a fool." I always grew extremely nervous whenever the old man addressed me, as though Robbie had some kind of spell going, some delicate configuration of words that would crumble if I spoke into it. "You get old either way," he said. "It can't be circumvented. You get old either way, so you'd best live whatever life gives for you to live."

"It's better," I said uncertainly, "to have something to care for. Is that what you mean?" But the old man spared me a response. He stared vaguely toward Robbie, who was flitting around the room they'd just carved up like a delirious bird. For six months I had been operating under the assumption that we were just taking this old man for a ride. But people can make all kinds of assumptions about a situation without really understanding it. After my exchange with the old man I felt anxious—unable, suddenly, to decode what foul propellants carried us. All morning this nervousness pulled on me, from the floor of my stomach down into my legs, flooding me with a kaleidoscope of violent cravings, and numbing all the sense I had.

"It is definitely time," Robbie said, smiling wildly, "to go get more lumber."

I went back to the attic to check on Baby. "Baby?" I called out, half expecting to find him unconscious. But he seemed to be handling things well up there—much better, in fact, than I ever had. I watched as he worked the wires over and under one another, like he was wrapping a present for someone, wielding the wire stripper and making thoughtful little snips with it. I had once watched this special about people who get hit in the head and then become geniuses, math savants and successful painters and all that, and I supposed this might be what had happened to Baby. One of the men on this special had been standing at a payphone in some park, talking to his mother—probably begging her forgiveness for something—when a bolt of lightning had plunged down out of a cloud and slammed into the telephone line, roaring through the phone and into his face and turning him into a famous composer. They had a neuroscientist on there to explain it. He said it used to be they thought, with one part busted up, the brain could devote more energy to other parts. But that wasn't really it, he said. He said that the damaged part of the brain—the part having to do with clear thinking and logic and all that—for that whole person's life had actually repressed the other parts, the artistic and inventive parts, which had really always existed there in those people, dormant and waiting. When one part got dulled down, in other words, the other could come free. Watching Baby work, I remembered all of this and longed at once for Robbie's cooler. If I moved quickly I could get to it before we went for lumber.

"Great work Baby!" I said, and hurried back out through the little attic scuttle, leaving him again.

Robbie was already at the truck when I got to it, and I knew I would have to wait for him to decide it was time to drink. He and I rode out through the twisting roads, past old barns and little berry farms until we reached a string of strip malls where the lumber store sat. Robbie parked as he always did, far from the other vehicles, at the very goddamn back of the vast parking lot, and not even in a real spot. Walking through the expanse of the lot, thrown again amongst the civilized, I had the unmistakable feeling that we were lost, irreparably misplaced, and that at any moment those around us would find out and we would be plunged down into the ground where we belonged. Inside, it took about half an hour to get what we needed. Robbie examined the pine studs thoroughly, speaking softly to each one.

"My darling," he whispered. "what a fine one you are." I waited and watched the people who passed us by. They were mostly older married couples, sweetly dressed and planning little weekend renovations on their homes. A few real contractors walked by too, meaty men whose hands looked to be chiseled out of granite and who clutched at their belts uncomfortably—men who really lifted things and set them back in new arrangements, who commanded chaos into order, rather than the other way. None of them deigned to look at us. Robbie was singing now to his lumber. "These arms of mine," he sang, "they are yearning! Yearning..."

"Robbie," I said under my breath. "We have to get the fuck

out of this place." Beneath the simmering lights of the store we seemed exposed, our skin more gray and our faces more hopeless than we'd realized. The light had revealed that we weren't really people at all, but some nocturnal little monsters that had stumbled through the automatic doors by accident, with no clue now how to leave. I guessed Robbie must have been oblivious to this reality, though it was plain. For my part I wanted to break something dear to these people, and I feared them and I hated them now more than ever. It felt crazy that anyone would want to light a place so as to exhibit this much. Robbie undid some sort of fastener, and then an avalanche of lumber fell down toward us so that we had to leap out of the way. "You fucking pillheaded maniac!" I said, and kicked at the new heap before us. "I'm going to go wait in the truck." My knowledge, as I left him, that his cooler was there in the truck bed gave me great new powers of impermeability, and I marched confidently out of the store, stuffing shiny little precision instruments into my pockets as I went.

I was feeling much better, sitting on a little grassy median in the parking lot beneath the shade of a pitiful tree, when Robbie walked up.

"Where," I wondered, "is the lumber?"

"I got it, I got it," he said. "But look." And I saw now he had something else. Bundled up in the bottom of his shirt, he showed me, Robbie cradled a corn snake.

"Jesus!" I said, and leapt away.

He said, "The pet shop next door had these in the window!" I stared at him a while. I was vaguely aware of the pet shop, which you could smell on your way into the lumber store—the kind of smell that should tell anyone with sense to stay away. I stepped forward again, carefully, and peered down into his shirt. The snake twisted slowly around itself in a single, concentrated clump. It was a vibrant and glassy orange, like the inside of a tangerine, and it knotted itself more and more tightly together. "He was only forty dollars." Robbie informed me. I tried but could not see the head within the writhing mass.

"What does it eat?" I asked.

"Sir John eats rodents," he said, somewhat indignantly.

"Isn't it poisonous? Aren't you afraid it will bite somebody?"

"Now!" he said. "What kind of a crazy asshole would I have to be to carry around a poisonous snake? Sir John's bite is harmless." I gazed again at the roiling orange in the bed of his shirt, transfixed. For a moment I felt as though I were peering down into a little campfire, one that Robbie somehow held. "Well," Robbie said, "let's load him into the truck." The snake meandered around on the bench seat while we heaved stuff into the bed. Then we got in and Robbie drove, the thing wrapped around his wrist as he did so, just as if it was some kind of infernal jewelry and he was the ferryman taking us away.

"Sir John!" he said, "you fucker, that tickles!" We ran a red light, and I could hear the car horns shrieking after us, their din dissolving swiftly under the force of Robbie's old truck. It seemed at any moment we might die and take all kinds of other things down with us. I felt giddy and light, like a child excited for a bedtime story, excited to drift off. The lumber shifted back and forth behind our heads, drumming out a primal measure. I let out a laugh. At some point the snake slid off of Robbie's arm and dropped down toward the pedals. He bent to grab it, keeping one hand on the steering wheel as he fished around at his feet, glancing now and again back up at the road. The truck's wheels gave a pained yip, and then we rose up into the air, where we seemed to stay, our bodies emptied of their weight. I felt then as though the snake had always been with us, as though it had only been waiting, like a certain breed of angel, for our greatest moment of want. The truck came down crooked, throwing me for a moment into the driver's seat before wrenching me away again. I could see now we were off the road, but only slightly. Nothing seemed broken. Robbie rose up from the floorboards gripping Sir John.

"Another plan come perfectly together," I said, as though from far above the scene. Robbie didn't reply. He only looked lovingly into the snake's secretive, pitiless little face.

We had left a trail of two-by-fours in the dirt behind us, as well as nails and blades and brackets and all sorts of other hard-to-see shit, and before pulling away we spent a long time on our hands and knees, trying to collect it all. A light rain began to fall on us. We couldn't say how much we'd lost there when we finally pulled off, only that we'd tired of looking.

"You didn't get lunch," the old man said, as we arrived. I'd half expected the whole house to have vanished when we pulled up—not demolished, simply gone. Robbie didn't want to introduce the old man to Sir John yet, I supposed, because he'd left him to bask in the warmth of the truck, the windows cracked in spite of the rain. He came in and began to explain things to the old man, pulling crumpled brown papers out of his pocket to reveal the floorplans he'd drawn in a crazed and fat-fisted hand. As Robbie buzzed around him, the old man moved into the kitchen, which we'd left mostly intact, and started a pot of water on the stove. I could not tell if he was really listening to Robbie. He took down a plastic cutting board from a half-dismantled cabinet and began to chop garlic, as casually as if we weren't even there, as if we'd never been there to begin with and had never torn away the room he now worked calmly in.

"How about a nice soup," he said.

"Fine," Robbie said. "Fine." And went on with his explanation. I walked out through the hallway and down toward the stairs.

It's probably best if I describe this house a little better, because it was important to us. It was important to me. I still wake up from dreams about that house, wake up sweating, in the kinds of places that humiliate you the moment you regain consciousness —a bus at the end of its route, or the couch of someone who's told you already to leave, or just wrapped up in your own, filthy bedsheets—wake up from dreams in which I'm moving carefully across the rafters, able to see each room below me perfectly. That house was important. Every other thing in my life, every other thing aside from that house, was already fucked, with no way whatsoever to be mended. Each day I would walk down the hall in boots that were too big, kicking up debris and dust which had once been the ceiling. All the dust rested over these panels of cardboard that Robbie had us tape down over the hardwood floors when we first came in, to protect them. Such a gesture of care astonished me. I wondered where he'd learned it.

When you go into a house, any house, you have no idea really what's in it. But the tradesman, the people who built the place, people who've been dead fifty years, they leave all sorts of things in the walls—glass bottles, old wooden toys, even letters—and it is sacrilege, so Robbie said, to remove any of it. And so each time we walked through the rooms we passed by the portals we had made, openings we'd blown out of the plaster with the claw of a hammer, which revealed these dark and otherworldly rooms within the walls, rooms only we knew, among all of the living. Everything you spend your life believing to be permanent, all the good and bad, turns out to be more brittle than a bone.

Feeling by then very heavy, I walked up the stairs, which had no railing anymore to protect me if I fell, and called out eagerly to Baby. I could hear the rain picking up outside. I called out again, my voice an embarrassing sound ringing back at me, and then I crawled halfway up into the attic. A lot of the wiring was done, I saw, the bright strands meticulously tacked up to the rafters in rich and geometric patterns. All the tools had been arranged in a neat pile in the corner, and Baby was gone. Illness flooded my body. "Baby!" I called out, stupidly. Half my body was in the attic, half below, and I was shining a little flashlight around frantically. For a moment I feared Baby had been some sort of a delusion. My grandfather, and also a couple of uncles, were locked away a long time for hearing voices, and it's always been a fear of mine to follow that tradition, to make friends with a misfire in my brain. I must have stood there a long time, worrying about this.

Eventually I crawled down out of the attic and went back to find Robbie and the old man. They were standing around a miter saw. Robbie was making little adjustments on the thing with a screwdriver, then cutting scraps of wood with it and cursing. There was a bowl of soup sitting beside him, which he hadn't seemed to have touched. The old man looked up at me when I entered.

"Baby is missing," I said. "Have you seen him?"

Robbie made one more cut on the saw, which let out a frenzied howl. "Sometimes he runs off," he said.

"What?"

"They told me when I got him the job," he said impatiently. "They said sometimes he runs off."

I stepped closer, wanting him to say more. "Well where does he go?" I insisted. The old man stood looking down at a framing square he held in his hand, clearly very puzzled by it.

"Oh I don't know," Robbie said. "Just away. Away. But then back. He always comes back." He was not looking at me. His tongue stuck out as he focused on his task. "And anyway," he added. "What are you so worried for? It's still the guy who threw that cinder block through your coffee table and stole your DVD player. Did you forgive all that already?"

It was true. Baby had done some bad things in the past. He was that guy, still, yet he was not. It didn't seem to be an issue of forgiving. "What should we do?" I asked.

"It's *fine*," Robbie said, and let the saw down with a slam. I could see now he'd had a few drinks too, when no one was looking. "I was getting kind of bored anyway," he added, "of the way things were around here." The drinks, as sometimes happened, were making him mean, and he was disappearing into something much smaller, much harder than himself, and down into a little chore. To see him this way always gave me the same feeling I got when I was little and my dad would drink, the feeling that something nightmarish was about to begin.

The old man looked at me blindly. His eyes seemed to glass over and he furrowed his brow, so that I worried he might have a stroke. "You'd better check the old greenhouse," he said, matter-of-factly.

Robbie looked up from his work. "What greenhouse," he said, irritated.

"Susan's," he said. "Out in the back." Behind the house there was a thick shroud of kudzu which I had always taken to be the end of the old man's property. Now the old man led me back there, the rain by then falling mercilessly on us. Robbie stayed inside and worked by himself, brooding, resentful of everything before him. It was very dark out because of the rain, and even darker as we got into the dense tangle of trees and vines. The old man held a heavy flat rake and he used it to tear away the kudzu, feebly, until I could see the glass structure behind it. The little building was made out of a lot of old and mismatched windows. Most of the panes had been shattered and the rain fell down through them and onto the dark and wild plant life inside. We shined flashlights in. There was no one. All the things inside of the damp little building—the broken pots on the shelves and the old bags of soil—had been thickly coated with the fur of some shedding animal, wild and brightly lit. The old man opened the door. "Susan loved to garden," he said, and stepped inside. It was not large enough for the two of us to stand in there together, and I watched him from the doorway. It became obvious at once that I should not be there. It was as though I was standing right in the old man's mind, and that my being there presented some great hazard to it. Everything in the space was composed of the same glimmering shade. I felt a sudden terror overcome me, an irratio- nal certainty that, now there, I would never be able to leave. The old man picked up a rag and stared into it, as though it projected for him a little film of his life. Overhead the water dripped through the cracked glass and down onto him. I stood watching, standing at the place that falls out beyond time. And what was he thinking, there in the dark recess of his past? I hoped never to know.

"We should probably get back," I said, hesitantly. The little building seemed to be one throbbing organ in which the old man was suspended, and I backed away, feeling as though any minute the whole thing would expand and swallow me.

"It would be best," he said softly, as if half-asleep, "if I stay here now." He still held the rake in one hand, like a sentinel on watch.

"Okay," I said, and continued to back away. "That's okay." I had no idea what in the fuck was happening. I began to walk back to the house as quickly as I could, almost running from the old man's sorrow. But somewhere inside of myself I knew something. I knew that there was no escaping it, that any direction I fled would flush me down into the same sad scene. This is just how being damned works. I could hear the saw howling in the distance, causing the lights inside the big house to flicker as it did so, and, sickly, I went toward that sound.

Inside, I avoided Robbie. The house was large enough that you could go a week without knowing someone else was in it with you, and I went from room to room, calling Baby's name. In one part of the house, we had undone the roof and only half replaced it with plywood and tarps, and here I had to walk through leaks and puddles, as well as a kind of paste the sawdust made when wet, and it was here too that the rain began to fall so heavily outside that I had to stop and stand there, listening. Sometimes it comes so hard you just have to surrender. For some reason then I thought of my mom, of her sitting out on her little stoop whenever it rained in the evenings, smoking and watching the streets fill up with that shimmering light. My mom, whose house I was no longer allowed to visit according to her boyfriend, because I'd come one day when no one was home, and forced a window and taken a few things off to be pawned. But that had been almost a year ago, and I still hoped, with the unique stupidity of a child, that the next time she saw me she might be proud. The rain died down some, and I started again to yell out for Baby, moving through the tarps that hung down all around me like the massive web of a spider. I was very afraid, and didn't even really know it.

"Baby!" I cried. "Baby!" That was when I heard some shouting. I ran through the house as quickly as I could in my oversized boots, ran as through a heavy flood, until I reached the room where Robbie worked. "What was that?" I asked.

"What," he said numbly. "What was what?" I didn't answer him. I went outside again, around to the back. I shined my little flashlight around, calling out to Baby. I heard a rustling. "Baby!" I said. And then I saw him. He was holding the old man's rake, and the old man lay before him in the grass.

It must have been twenty times I heard Baby explain what had happened, the same each time, down to the detail. And I believed him, of course. Not that it mattered. But why wouldn't I believe him. He was a good person. I saw enough to see that. He was a good person and it didn't have to happen like it did. Not to him.

What happened, he said, was after he'd done a few hours of work in the attic he went outside to get some air. It was always so hot in the attic. He thought we would have been back by then, Robbie and I, but we weren't, so he decided to go for a walk. The weather that day was nice for summer, it hadn't yet started to look like rain, and he wanted to walk out there in the country, where there were hardly any cars going by, and he could hear all the birds. When he got back—it was raining hard by then—he stopped to get some things out of the truck, a rain jacket and a smoke, and that was when he'd met the snake—Sir John, curled up still in the floorboards. He thought it was wild, the snake. How could he know it was a pet? He thought it had come up from underneath the truck, through some kind of gap in the fire-wall. That had happened once when he was a kid, he said, with a family of rats in a Bronco. Baby wasn't afraid of the snake, but he wanted to set it free, so he picked it up, carefully, and carried it out to the back of the house. The old man, of course, was in the middle of his fever dream—I knew that—and I guess he must have gotten very frightened when he saw Baby there, such a tall figure holding a big bright snake out in front of him. It was dark, very dark for that time of day, and Baby said the old man shouted at him, menaced just as though Baby had been an intruder. The old man still had the rake, the flat rake in his hands, and before Baby could really talk to him, he took it and started to swing it at him, and there was a kind of struggle between them, and the old man took a strike across the face with the rake, and he fell down. They said later that the cause of death had been a trauma induced heart attack. Of course we didn't know what to do. The old man wasn't breathing, and we were scared.

Baby was a good person. I knew he was telling us the truth. He was crying, for god's sake. But Robbie said it didn't matter. We were a handful of addicts without any kind of contractor's license or recorded experience, no paperwork at all aside from past criminal charges. And Robbie said if we called the police we would all go down, and I guessed he was probably right. He had a gift for calculating things out like that. But there was no record, he said, of he or I having worked there for the old man. All anyone had was our first names, and he said we could just leave, that no one would track it back to us. But the same wasn't true for Baby. When we'd gotten him the job, there was all this paperwork his sister had filled out, with the old man's name and address and everything on it. And Robbie's idea was that we leave Baby there, that we had no choice, in fact. He couldn't be helped.

Well, Robbie was half right. They certainly connected it back to Baby, but of course they also linked it back to us—all the checks the old man had written us, I figure. Robbie and I did a few years on fraud and a couple other minor offenses, and I never saw him again after that. But they sent Baby away for a very long time, sent him to the place where he is still, the kind of place that makes your skin crawl just to think of, where all they have to eat is haldol, crayons and white bread.

෨

I will never as long as I live forget the look on Baby's face as we drove off. "Please," he was saying to me. "I'm sorry. Please..." His huge face was so mangled by sorrow and fear, and he wept like a giant child, soaking wet. We were all drenched. Whatever in life gave me any sort of courage, I was leaving the last of it behind that day. And as we pulled away I tried not to look, but he ran desperately after us, even clinging onto the tailgate for a few moments, sobbing, pleading after us—the rain falling down like the fulfillment of an omen. "Don't panic," Robbie was saying, dimly. "We'll figure something out." But I knew this was not true. The downpour and the groaning engine grew louder. I looked back at the house in the mirror, which would never now be finished, which would fill up with rain and fall away, and I knew we would not have anything more to strive for. And Baby. He was kneeling there in the driveway, like a child in the mud, vanishing behind us as we went. In those last seconds before the whole scene disappeared, I watched him. That is the image I can still remember. Baby's face was drained of panic then, almost like he was at peace. It was only loss left, what I saw on Baby's face— pure and simple loss—and I knew from then on it would be this sight, unceasingly, I would come to face.

HOW COME ALL THE SCHOOLS SHUTTED DOWN

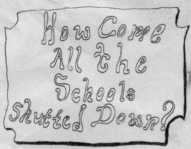

How Come All the Schools Shutted Down?

a guide for children living in the end times

Hello! Are you feeling very *very* sad lately?

Has the mail stopped arriving at your parent's house? Do you worry about the **feral dogs** that flood the city streets? Do you sometimes find your mommy or daddy sitting in the bathtub, **sobbing**? Do you wonder why everyone is standing in the streets **shouting**? Or do you simply miss the birds?

Well, if these or similar issues trouble you, you're not alone. **Sadness**, **fear**, and feelings of **profound futility** are all perfectly acceptable emotions for a child living here in **the final days of the empire**. It's important to recognize first that it's **not your fault**.

Growing up can be tough for anyone, and when geopolitical meltdowns result in the vague glow of **desperation** and **paranoia**, it can seem downright unfair. But there's no reason you can't be happy in these final few weeks (or months) of civilization as we know it. After all, everyone deserves to have a **childhood**.

Here are just a few things you might keep in mind, to help accept the **shattered** state of mankind:

1. DEATH is a natural part of life. As the **hoards** grow increasingly **angry**, forcibly enter your home, and rummage through your kitchen, remember that such **consolidation of resources** is only the

1

briefest impediment to the forces of hunger known as **mortality**. Think about it this way, when was the last time you heard **laughter** coming from one of those marauding **citizen-militias**? It is difficult to enjoy those stolen FEMA ration boxes when you never stop to taste them.

In the time that you have here on Earth, consider cultivating an attitude of **acceptance**. There is nothing any better for you elsewhere. So consider this time a gift.

2. MOMMY and DADDY can't help you. No one can. This situation is unfortunately out of their hands. That doesn't mean that **they don't love you**.

3. ANGER only deepens your suffering. Life can be **frustrating**. Sometimes you just want to go outside and play with your friends, but they've all been taken away by groups of men in black **riot gear**, and you have to play inside today because the sun's **radiation** causes our **skin to fall off**. Who wouldn't be upset?

Nevertheless, all the anger in the world cannot change **civilization's** exponential rate of **decay**. For you and those around you (be it in a nearby **bomb-shelter** or the dark corridors of that "temporary" **holding center**) it may be in your interest to remain positive. Be a source of light: tell a few jokes to the night-guard on duty at your local settlement or encampment; smile at the **Google Observer** when he or she comes to assess the viability of potential **Neo-Citizens**; pick the **trash** up off the ground, even if more will only pile up there tomorrow. Of course none of this will in any way fix **the problem**. It will only improve the conditions, sometimes.

4. UNDERSTANDING is an illusion. Try to imagine how the family pet felt, shortly before **the contagion** spread throughout the country. Do you think poor Rufus was lying in his **doggy bed** night after night dreading the inevitable near-future wherein he would have to be put down due to the **violent and all-consuming virus** coming closer and closer to his city, and thus his nervous-system? Perhaps. Perhaps not. But think: which would you like to *hope* that he experienced? That's right! **Peaceful ignorance!** And the same can be said

2

about you! The more information we have about this world we live in, the more **disoriented** and **bewildered** we become. This makes it hard to focus on anything beyond **the irreparable human predicament.** And that's no way to live.

5. <u>The total ENTROPY of an isolated system can never decrease over time.</u> In the past, kids your age did not have to grapple with a concept like **the vital second law of thermodynamics.** But those days have passed. If we are to accept anything, we must first accept this.

Remember the last time you built a sand-castle in your **district ash-dump?** When you came back the next day, I'll bet your castle had vanished. This is known as **entropy. Entropy** is an energetic system's natural preference toward, and gradual decline into, **disorder** and **degeneration.** When the **acid rain** washed away your sand-castle, you witnessed **entropy** at work. The idea of **irreversibility** is central to the understanding of **entropy.** You can never **unscramble the egg.** Like it or not, the world we live in is supremely governed by this law. All life is at last subject to **entropy.**

If you're ever having trouble keeping any of these ideas in mind, just think of the acronym **A.R.T.I.S.T.S.,** which is short for:

Accepting the Radical Turmoil
Interred Senselessly in our Transitory Souls

If this doesn't help, little else will. Though it is still a good idea to wear **sun-screen,** avoid **irradiated** canned-goods, and *never* talk to **strangers.**

For additional literature on the end of life, write to the address below.

FOR FREE DISTRIBUTION—NOT TO BE SOLD
Artists United in Ending
3416 6th st Apt 1
Tuscaloosa, Alabama 35401 U.S.A.
e-mail: artistsunitedinending@gmail.com

3

DELIVERY

Beautiful, moronic men huddle together chanting indecipherable things toward a television, which they've dragged onto the porch. They drink desperately from little cans that nearly disappear into their fists and speak in brutal riddles.

"Bro," says one, "I'm gonna fuckin slam you in your fuckin eye right now bro."

"Bro chill," says another. "Damn." Taken from a distance, it is difficult to speak to any individual imperatives among them. These men, in truth, have always been here, standing as they do with blank and swollen stares, their laughter indiscernible from their screams, their minds made full by yawning blood. Yes, these men have been here always, though the bodies come and go like water in a bog. Everywhere the tremor of their actions rings and this, it seems, means almost nothing to them.

When the dog arrives it does so easily, like a dart thrown through smoke, and disperses for a time whatever has possessed these men, for at once they lower themselves and speak softly to it. It licks at their faces, as happy to see them as it is to see anything.

"Whoa!" say the men. "What a sweet little pup! What a good dog!" And it is. It is a very good dog, and the world, as a result, is good to it, is realized in its gaze. Through the dog's damp eyes the men are born. Through its wet black nose they are delivered, for an instant, to the new life.

Softly, they huddle about the dog and pet it, seeking only the places it likes to be touched. "What's your name little guy?" they say, stroking it. "You got a tag?" The dog rolls onto its back, over-joyed. It has wandered from its yard in search of sick sweet smells, has followed the call issued out by all things and arrived at these men—who bury themselves in their fears—arrived and unfastened them. For the world, in this moment, is the dog's to inherit. "He's so soft!" the men murmur. "Where'd you come from, pooch?"

"Is it a boy dog or a girl dog?" asks another, though already the dog has lifted itself and moved on, voyaging through the doorway of the beleaguered house in which these men reside and discover-ing, there upon the coffee table, a glowing box of pork-fried rice. The grace this affords the dog, on being eaten, is unspeakable.

One of the men follows the dog inside and, seeing the mess of food spread over the carpet, begins to scold it. "*Bad* dog," says the man, the sound of which immediately floods the dog with nausea and with discord. The voice echoes deep into the dog and persists there, causing everything to tilt and twist upon itself. Naturally, the dog flees, scrambling with desperation—for just as the dog's way can radiate so too can the man's—out through the back door, and into another situation.

All the night before the dog has dreamed of snow, cool and silvery against its tongue. It has forgotten the dream, but still the sense of snow against its tongue remains. In a deserted alleyway the dog explores a while, then defecates. The sun is high and warm in the sky and covers the scene in its light. Into the alley someone has dumped from its pot a dying colocasia, and now the dog is diligently eating all the soil from its roots. Each act the dog performs becomes the only act. Each muscle in its body full with purpose.

Nearby a couple argues. The dog pauses its chewing and listens, dirt glistening on its rubbery lips. The voices are feverish and nasty and build toward an untenable pitch. The dog boofs once, in an effort to stop them, but the voices go on.

"No it's fucking not," says one. "No it is not! It's a respect thing Steven. You act like such a fucking asshole all the time! It's pretty fucking obvious you don't give a shit about me, or anyone else but your *clients*."

"I'm so fucking sick of your bullshit," says the other. "You don't ever listen. You don't ever fucking listen! You're too fucking damaged to hear anything I'm saying through your fucking paranoid delusions."

The two are not visible. Still their words, like the debris from some unfinished building, tumble out from them in all directions. The dog gives another bark, this one more insistent, and begins to run in their direction, determined to stop them. It bays brightly as it runs, throwing all of itself into the gesture. When it reaches them it finds them seated in a small rose garden hemmed in by tall boxwoods. Proudly the dog barks toward the two of them, wagging its high tail. The bark cascades ecstatically into yet one more careening bay and then, discovering its own uncertainty, the dog stops and waits.

"What the fuck?" says the man.

The woman brightens, holds out her hands. "Hello there," she says. The dog drops its ears and sniffs at the air between them, sensing in it something powerful. "Hey sweet girl," says the woman. "Where'd you come from?" At once the dog goes to her, just as it has gone for all of time and far beyond, goes and is gone in its going. "Hi sweet girl," she says again, and takes the dog into her arms. Though her voice feels frail and though her limbs feel weary she is immensely vivified.

"Whose dog is that?" asks the man.

The woman is sickened to remember the man's presence there beside her. "How would I know," she says to him, without looking up. The sick feeling makes way again for the dog, which nuzzles itself under her chin and moans gratefully. The dog too, for the moment, has forgotten the existence of the man, so small is his way in the face of this union. The woman runs her nails along the dog's soft back. A brilliance rests between them. "Where's your tag sweet girl?" she says.

"So what," the man says, "you're just done talking now?" Inside of him there is a bright black fire which consumes him, and which licks greedily against the borders of his being.

"What do you want me to do," says the woman, "throw her back out into the street?"

"Whatever," he says, and disappears into the large brick house. The dog watches him tentatively as he rises, relaxing only once he's out of sight. It lays its head in the woman's lap and splays its legs, wholly absorbed in the quietude between them. When, after a time, sleep finally arrives, it seems to do so from below, rising up like steam to meet the dog. In the dream it is running through a wood. All around are others like it, running. The slender tree limbs thrust themselves toward the dog, so that it must dart around them as it passes. Up ahead is a crystalline squirrel, which the dog pursues devotedly. Light falls through the squirrel as through a chandelier and shatters out. At once the wood opens into a valley and the squirrel is gone and the others too. Now there is a dim gray van that idles there before the dog, out of which someone appears. They are unbearably tall, and composed of only shadow, born of the places where light has not been. They reach one of their long, horrible arms toward the dog and it wakes.

The house is very still inside, though far from calm. Slowly from its place atop the couch the dog rises, unfurling its being out into the space. The walls are decorated rationally—cold track lighting and furniture of jagged, disorienting construction and austere gray color fields produced by artists of distinction. Taken together the space reveals itself to be an altar of control, though the dog notes only its stillness.

From the den and down the hollow corridor the dog wanders uneasily. It sniffs at the air but finds it baffling and blank. In another room there looms elaborate machinery with which the man builds all his muscle. This room, unlike the others, sings with the caustic scent of cleaner and gives the space the sense of having borne some kind of carnage.

A pair of leather shoes sit in the corner, reeking of life. These the dog makes for directly, taking one up into its mouth and lovingly thrashing it. In play, the spirit blossoms and bursts forth. The dog carries the shoe back into the hallway and races along with it, utterly enraptured. It whips it against the walls and watches the thrilling bounce it gives back, then lifts it again and bounds toward the kitchen, whereupon a kind of tryst begins between the two, the dog gnawing tenderly upon the shoe, and the shoe giving forth its complicated flavor.

For some time they lie there in this manner, their heat receding slowly through the cool white kitchen tile. And then there is a sound, a great stiffening slam which surges through the house and lifts the dog upright. Footsteps, like some inverted aftershock, swell up and move in toward the dog.

Even before the man speaks his arrival produces a cloud of

distortion and throws the world into a wicked light. "This is not fucking happening," is what he says, and disappears again. When he returns a moment later he is holding a cold-cut of salami in one hand and a pink restraint in the other. Still the cloud is there, causing all the air to throb arrhythmically.

"Here girl," he says, "come here girl," and begins to approach the dog. The dog scampers away and attempts without success to dematerialize beneath a dinner table, before darting again in another direction. But the man reaches the dog regardless—for in this place there are only corners—and after some struggle he has the dog tied by the neck. Ruthlessly he drags the dog toward him, though nature finds their nearness wholly repellent. "Good dog," he says, and presses the cold-cut up to its lips, though the dog is too dumb with fear to respond. Then he drags it outside and into the car, which he fires up and drives off in.

On his way the man displays a truly fine command over the intricate machine and, too, a first-rate sense of discipline, for he travels just over the limit.

At the shelter he decides he won't go in. Instead he leaves the engine running and comes around to the passenger-side, where he pulls the dog out and ties it up to a nearby chain-link fence. There is a moment, before he departs, when the man stands over the dog, regarding its existence with imperiousness, as though through some dense veil. Then he gets into his car and he leaves.

If only somehow, on being taken to this shelter and diverging from that man, the dog at last could be relieved from such an abstruse hell as this. If only it could, through the mystery's sweet mercy, be freed from the twisted jurisdiction it has found itself in. But the pitiful truth is this: the man was nothing more than one apostle of this fearful way, of which there are unnumbered others. And, worse still, they have together built out such a bitter wilderness that violent institutions of control must be perpetually installed, in order to protect against the constant threat imposed by those already operating. It is this contorted vale through which each soul must navigate, and the dog is no exception.

In the dying sun it sits and waits. Slowly, the resolution of the world returns, revealing, among other things, the truly anguished cries that pour forth from this dim decaying shelter. With sudden, anxious urgency the dog begins to chew upon its flank—a gesture much the same as the reverberation that an object yields on being struck. The dog sinks its teeth in with total abandon, uprooting small tufts of its fur. It is not an itch exactly, but something else that screams atop the skin and begs to be annihilated, some hopeless impulse to destroy the self that suffers, to deny somehow the state in which the dog has found itself. Some, it has been said, are born into this endless night. Others are delivered to it. Still some turn their denial outward, and pitch their homes into this lightless flame as best they can. That is their choice. But a great many people, and surely more than can be proven, strive every hour to enact that other, brighter world, which they can see so clearly and which, as always, lives.

By the time a large sedan enters the parking lot it has grown dark out, and the headlights send a tremble through the dog. From out of the vehicle climbs a child, playfully hopping along on one foot and followed in a moment by her grandmother, who steps with great care. Watching them, the dog is overtaken all at once with yearning, which lifts it to its feet and surges out by way of plaintive whines. "Oh sweetheart," the old woman says, "I think that doggy already belongs to someone." But the little girl has stopped in her tracks to gaze at it. There is something transfixing in the space that separates them, something which the child just faintly can detect. "Come along dear," says the old woman, "there'll be lots to choose from when we get inside," and, taking the child by the hand, recedes into the building.

Eagerly, the dog sits down, awaiting their return.

INTERVIEW WITH
THE POPE

The Pope had written the words: "Clear enough behind soft white smiles: the tongue. And beyond that: the breath. And beyond that? Nothing."

But when asked what he had meant by this, he said very little. He chewed the inside of his cheek. He wanted us to guess.

The Pope (he asked me to call him Tomás but I declined his offer) recalled his youth for me. "I was a magnificent dancer," he said, "back in Flores." He took a sip of his tea. "The women loved for me to sway them through the bars and out into the night."

"The women?" I asked.

At noon he ate a salad with a ginger ale, out on his patio. His assistants clustered about him, watching the artful stillness of his body, the immense breaths between bites. I sat at the table with him. He asked me about God, about all God's secrets. I guess I wanted to impress him, to surprise him. I told him that God loved rot and rust especially, that they were his first-borns, his most natural laws. The Pope stirred his drink with his pinky finger and did not look up when I'd finished speaking.

"Can I bum one of those?" he asked, pointing to the pack of cigarettes I'd brought. I slid them over. I was very nervous. Before flying in for this interview I'd been part-time at K-WLX for the last year, but still I needed to work four days a week at RadioShack. Holly told me The Pope was our ticket out of poverty. But sitting there with him now, watching him smoke one of my Winstons, I felt uncomfortable regarding him in this way. "Thank you," The Pope said, and blew a sheet of white into the air. "Ask me something?"

Sometimes, when an interview was going either very well or very poorly, I caught myself drawing on my notes. The drawings looked like this:

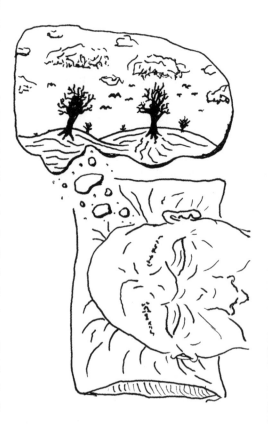

I looked up from my legal pad. My mind twisted in my head and my heart raced (I have a condition), but I retained my composure and asked my next question. "Do you feel, when you're lying in bed each night, like you have missed out on something important?"

The Pope smiled at once. He leaned back, draped an arm over the back of his chair. "I feel," he said, taking a deep drag and letting it out, "as if long ago I dove into the crisp water, and that now as I swim through this clean, clear water, I sometimes fail to feel the sun in its full force, or to hear the chants the birds all carry. Some things I cannot meet from where I sit." Whenever he spoke he stroked the arm of his chair, as though that were his way of learning the world. "But you understand this. Your expression is: one foot in and one foot out. Isn't it?"

I thought about Holly, the snow of her body laid out across the bed, which with a touch became possessed with pink. Certain extraordinary suffering sends one leaping from the boat. Every night one of us wept, either she or I, though sometimes both. I felt monstrous letting us go on like that. But we were in love.

The Pope's smoke went out, so I relit it for him. He gave a great sigh. The cool air of the morning had dissipated, and the sun swelled to reveal a spectacle of wounds dashed across the old man's face. In such light, the white of his skullcap and robe had become furious and blinding.

I tried to ask another question: "Would you say," I asked, "that you had a normal childhood?—Relatively speaking?" His assistants had brought out a large steel oscillating fan which clicked back and forth beside him, causing every ten seconds his wide white eyebrows to flutter.

"I fell ill a lot," he said. "As a child, my eyelids would crust together in my sleep. When I awoke, I'd be unable to open them. Sometimes I had to sit in that darkness for hours. My mother would take my hand and guide me to the sink, where she had prepared a bowl of warm water to pour over my eyes. My mother pouring bowl after bowl, to soften them up."

One of the assistants sneezed. The Pope smiled, still looking down at the table.

"She sounds very kind," I said, but he seemed not to hear me. He thumbed the petals of the centerpiece carefully: a heap of dusk-colored jacarandas pouring up from a thin white vase. The

Pope lifted the vase. He tipped it back and forth, slowly, allowing bits of water to dribble away. The contents were not afraid.

He wondered aloud, "How do they get them that color?"

Together we watched the flowers, which trembled now and then in tandem with his hand. He held them up to the light, allowing the petals their translucence.

"Must be a dye," he said sadly, and set them down again.

I noticed that something had shifted in his assistants, their body language had stiffened and they had begun glancing at each other fretfully. I persisted with the interview.

"And growing up, who would you say was your greatest hero?"

He popped the tip of his cigarette against the leg of the table—pop, pop; like that—to extinguish it. "I think it would be best if we went to the swimming hole for the remainder of this interview," he said, running his finger across his jawline. And then he said, "We're not so good at goodbyes yet, are we?" and rose from his seat, prompting the swarm of assistants to suddenly scatter.

The last time I'd left the country, I brought Holly with me. I'd been assigned a story on the drug cartel, and together we had driven down to Guadalajara. There, a faint longing hung everywhere. Holly bought me a candle, I remember, depicting Christ in pain. She bought me several chocolates, which we ate while stuck in traffic. I was telling Holly about my dream, I remember. Along the roads, children would knock on our windows, trying to sell us tissue boxes for 25 pesos. The tissue boxes too depicted Christ in pain. At one point, we came upon a boy who did not seem to want any money. He stood at an intersection, screaming at the sky. The sky could not hear him. His voice got caught in the ugly heights of the buildings.

"Then the dream ends with me meeting my hero," I said.

"Which one?"

"Gerard Manley Hopkins."

"The actor?" she asked.

"No."

"But why were you climbing the tree?"

"I was feeding bubblegum to the ants." We had been sitting at the red light for what felt like half an hour. Holly dropped the car into neutral, and the engine idled low.

The boy stood right outside my window, screaming. Although the sun was out, a slight rain fell like static over everything.

"I don't think anyone actually knows you," Holly said to me suddenly. The boy went on screaming. Strands of his hair thrashed against his forehead.

"Well, actually," I said, "actually, I'm intimate with lots of people. All kinds of people, willing to share themselves with me."

"Necesito sobrevivirme!" the boy screamed, "Necesito sobre-vivirme!" which I understood to mean, 'I need to survive myself,' but could not make sense of beyond the simple act of translation.

"Though I do lie to myself," I said. "Almost every day I find I'm lying to myself." Holly smiled blankly at me. She was unwilling to understand, would not spend the effort. "Holly?" I said.

I looked out at the boy one last time before the light turned green. Thin, white lacerations were spilled across his face like nails along a hardwood floor. The sunlight collected in his over-sized t-shirt, and turned him into a paper-lantern. He went on screaming, his voice curling about the savage wires of that city.

The Pope, small in stature and gifted all over with dents, glided through the hum of spring. Jagged olive trees wended along the walkway, hunched and marred by the years of pruners who'd cut them from the path.

The Pope had, by that time, made a lot of changes to the palace. Many were upset by his decisions to fire the in-house butcher and tear down all the window blinds.

He leaned toward me as we walked. "L'uragano," he said. "Around here they have this nickname for me."

At the swimming hole, the assistants had already set up several white umbrellas and deckchairs before we'd arrived, as well as a rolling cart which held a stack of phonograph records and a small wooden victrola. Large drops of sun fell through the trees.

"The weather's so nice today," I said.

He didn't respond. He touched the horn of the victrola, brass painted around the rim with little white morning glories. "Do you like Bach?" he asked. He shuffled his records for a time, then put on something else, some compromise he'd made with himself, which seemed not to please anyone exactly. "As a child I sometimes sang instead of sobbing," he said, "My mother approved of this, and did her best to keep me at it. But the war held us all by the throat for so very long." He closed his eyes.

"The war—" I began.

"Nevertheless!" he said, and this word he pronounced quite slowly, and with great intention, "Music is the wind within the hurricane! In the end it cannot be vanquished by means of fire, only made more ferocious." He held his hands high in the air, as though he were a conductor. They remained raised long after he'd finished speaking, craggy fingers pointing up to something, eyes closed tightly the whole time. Then he looked out at the body of water. "They told me it would be good cardiovascular training," he said, and removed his robe and hat, revealing swim shorts underneath.

The Pope had no jewelry, only a ribbon which he kept always tied around his wrist. It was pink and tattered, faded very badly at one end. He told me a little girl in Sierra Leone had given it to him, ten days before dying of an easily curable illness. "That girl understood darknesses I will never be able to imagine," he told me. "Such shadows are woven through the bloodstream of even fragile angels such as her. I keep this always, to remind myself of her face, of all the things I cannot know."

Holly did not believe in God, and I had never thought to tell her that I did. The night before I left, she told me my temperament was milk-warm.

"Milk-warm?" I said. "Is that the expression?" She told me that when we went out to places, restaurants and bars, I never talked to anyone.

"I'm tired of having to smile at the waitress for the both of us," she said.

For the past week, she had refused to sleep in the bedroom with me. Every night except one, when she'd curled into a ball and let me hold her til she twitched to sleep. I laid awake that night and thought of dying, of how calm it must be.

I sat by the water in the navy blue tie and the shoes I'd bought for this trip. The Pope played in the water nearby, giggling at the way the splashes rose and fell onto his skin. He floated on his back for several minutes, long enough that his assistants began to grow anxious. He spoke as he floated toward me, without opening his eyes. "What ails you, my child?"

"Nothing," I said, "Nothing does."

"No one really knows you," he said. Then he said, "The lips become a nest for all the things we can not say," and began swimming in tight circles, which gradually increased in size. Then, he stopped and, grinning, splashed me. "Bock, bock?" he asked coyly. The water bled into my dress-shirt and cooled my body.

"Do you ever wish God could advise you directly?" I asked.

His feet emerged and vanished over and over. "You know, I have a pacemaker. You really shouldn't get me so worked up about Him." Then he said, "I insist you try this. It's divine," and spit a bit of water out.

"Okay."

"Wonderful!" He said, and powered toward the center of the water.

Facing away from him, away from all the assistants, I slid my clothes over my body and left them in the pit of a rock. As I stepped toward the water, the silt beneath my feet sank away, shrinking me by an inch and a quarter. Then I leapt in, ripping the water apart with my limbs. I surfaced, and found The Pope right next to me. The leaves in the trees seemed to applaud.

"Wonderful!" He said again. "Wonderful." He stood and watched himself in the warped surface of the water. After a moment, he said softly, "Eventually we give the body away, one way or another." A gasp from the assistants, as a branch floated past him. Why did his smile seem to come from outside himself, I wondered.

So close to him, I saw for the first time a copper colored scar, draped over his shoulder and hanging down his back. It curled finally up his neck and disappeared behind the ear. I tried to imagine him as a kid with a rifle, crouched in a trench and pleading with God. I thought of asking about the war, but I didn't. I laid down on the surface of the water and I hummed to the distant music. I watched the heavens spread out above me, and thought to myself: half the world is made of sky. The clouds appeared to wrinkle against the wind. The trees lashed the sky like inverse lightning. Here is how it looked:

Every branch straying from itself in static ecstasy, and the sun writing poems on the leaves.

"Isn't it almost dinner time?" The Pope asked, but I pretended not to hear him. The sky was a rind of sun falling. I imagined what it would sound like, if I were close enough to the sun to hear it, the rush of red thunder, like a boiling lake.

Walking back to the palace, a sudden wind swept through us, catching The Pope's hat and lifting it high into the air. Up in the sky it looked just like a kite. Several of his assistants ran after it, and when it finally landed they fought over it, tacitly, so as not to let him see their fighting. The one who finally ripped it away from the others—a tall, gaunt man—brought it to The Pope and bowed, smirking.

"Yes, my child," The Pope said, but handed the hat back to him and kept walking. We came to the entrance of the palace. Overhead, the night built up like a cough, and seemed to place us in another world entirely.

"Daniel," The Pope said, turning to this assistant, "prepare a room for our guest, please." The assistant glowered at me, and then turned and entered the palace. The Pope said, "I'll show you your room," but I did not know what to say. I certainly hadn't expected to stay here in the palace. I'd booked a hotel room for the next three nights. But The Pope smiled warmly, and I followed him inside.

On the morning I'd left for the trip, Holly made me breakfast and tried to apologize. "Stop crying. Please," she had said. "Stop." She poured me another cup of coffee and then, into that, the cream. She did this very slowly, trying to fill it all the way to the lip of the cup without it overflowing. I touched the soft, swollen marks on my cheek. The night before she had thrown a drink in my face, a vodka on the rocks, and the ice had somehow left my face littered with tiny pink scratches.

We sat and we watched the coffee, the way the white clouds encircled themselves and converged into gray at the center. I could see vibrations on the surface, from our breathing. Then the coffee dribbled over and pooled on the tablecloth. "Damn it!" she said, and rose to get a hand towel.

That same morning, outside the airport, I had nearly stepped on a bird, huddled in the middle of the sidewalk. She appeared to be asleep, and stood with her head bowed into her breast, her little eyes closed. I knelt down beside her, to get a better look. All the feathers had fallen from her face, leaving an infant pink behind. I blew on her, in case she was dead. She trembled lightly, but kept her eyes closed. Her wings were ruffled and gray, though they came to a sudden blue tip. Rather than sleeping, she seemed to be waiting.

A janitor came up behind me and pulled out one of his earbuds. "It's dead?" he asked me, and knelt down beside me, removing his rubber gloves.

"It's breathing," I said. Immediately, and in a gesture that never would have occurred to me, the janitor calmly held out a finger to the bird—and the bird, as if mesmerized, climbed onto the finger without opening her eyes. The janitor raised the bird up to eye-level. We watched the sun cast a golden film over her body. She shuddered and hiccupped. Then the bird opened her eyes, and looked at both of us. Something clicked in her and she panicked, took flight—but a jagged, weary flight, lurching and much too low to the ground. Her body thumped into the wind-shield of a nearby car. She sat there a moment, stunned, and then took off again, disappearing into the trees.

"I guess it's not ready," the janitor said, and put his gloves back on.

At nine o'clock, everything becomes quiet. Hundreds of night-lights line the palace halls, and with a single flick The Pope ignites them all. Together they cast the most feathery blue glow. The Pope wears his long red nightshirt, which looks very much like the white robes he's worn all day except that, against the red of the cloth, his face seems very pale, a rush of blue at each of his temples.

There are times when Holly asks me questions without answers. Times when dark circles form beneath her loving eyes.

Though there are more important things to think of now, I remind myself. How does The Pope feel about the current unrest in Venezuela? I ask him. "I feel," he begins, "that we are all part of the sputtering surface of a single great fire, and we long to return to the explosive depths of silence." I believe him, although he has missed a button on his pajamas.

"Do you want to hear a story?" he asks.

"Alright," I say.

"Wonderful!" He bounces on his heels and walks over to a bookshelf. Two of the shelves, I realize, are devoted to picture-books. He pulls one from the shelf, a book called *The Tawny Scrawny Lion.* He puts on a pair of eyeglasses and tells me to sit on the rug.

"Once!" he begins, "there was a tawny, scrawny, hungry lion who *never* could get enough to eat." From down here on the rug, I can see The Pope's bare feet peeking out from beneath his nightshirt. I am sure I had more questions for The Pope, but at the moment they escape me. "He chased monkeys on Monday, kangaroos on Tuesday, zebras on Wednesday, bears on Thursday, camels on Friday, and on Saturday, *elephants!*" He turns the book around to show me the pictures. They look like this:

"The other animals didn't feel safe. They stood at a distance and tried to talk things over with the Tawny, Scrawny Lion." The Pope runs his fingers over an illustration, which makes a *shhh* sound. "Just then, a fat little rabbit came hopping through the forest, picking berries. All the big animals looked at him and grinned slyly. 'Rabbit!' they said. 'Oh you lucky rabbit! We appoint you to talk things over with the lion.'"

I can see, when he holds the book out for me, that The Pope bites his nails a lot. "Well," The Pope continues, "that made the little rabbit feel very proud. 'What shall I talk about?' he asked eagerly. 'Oh any old thing,' said the big animals. 'The important thing is to go right up close.' So the fat little rabbit hopped right up to the big hungry lion and counted his ribs."

When I arrive at home again, I can hardly withstand life, the raw responsibility of living it. Holly has been well in my short absence. She makes herself a smoothie every morning now, and goes for long jogs at sunrise. Her strides are powerful, and by the heat she seems entirely unbothered. She tells me, after I have been home several days, that she has been painting, a massive painting that rests in our garage, which I am not yet allowed to look at. Her self-possession frightens me. I smile at her.

One day, I will grow up. It is not impossible to do so. Holly will be gone by then, of course, will have moved on to some other kind of loving, one in which her beloved's illness does not interlock with hers so finely. This is not unlikely. My growing will come only once we've parted, I suspect. At any rate it is a possibility.

MARIA

I

Tumbling through the little girl's skull, a cascade of lightning bugs so thunder-thick they make her heart hurt. "And why," she wonders, "are there so many cruel hairy men in this town?"

She goes to the park at 11pm. She is a tough little girl, does not need permission to act in this world. So she wanders through the dark playground until she meets the swing-sets. There, the creaking brings her up from Earth. It is hard coming up, beginning this life as a lump of cells in pink applause, arriving finally at this vanishing point just beyond dusk. And still, they expect her to go to *school* in the morning.

Tumbling, tumbling, bugs through the skull. Tomorrow she is to give a presentation on the evolution of the eye. "The eye," she will tell the other children, "is the result of pure chaos." No one will clap, at the end. They will be too surprised. No matter, such things as this world were not made for the little girl. Already she is weary of it all.

At home, it is the same as when she left. The dog's tail thwacks the floor three times, but he does not get up. So heavy with meat and age, always waiting for the door to open and for death to walk through, smiling and holding out treats. He has dreamed, three nights in a row, of a field of thick and untouched snow, of romping through this soft white erasure. But he does not remember any of his dreams. They drift up and out of him just after conception, as with any sensation in this life.

The little girl is called Maria. "Hello Ruckus," she says to the dog. "Don't tell anyone I was gone." But this is a joke between her and the dog, since neither of her parents would ever notice her absences. Ruckus gives one more thwack with his tail and gazes at her with his pure adoration.

✳

Maria sits on the school bus. It is only 6:45am, and all the night before she stayed awake constructing a great towering sculpture in her bedroom. Chicken wire and wet newspaper, up to the ceiling. It had come to her in an instant, appeared in her mind and set her hands to work. She had pulled the roll of wire in from the darkness, through the back door, dragged it up the stairs, as though she were possessed. She thought this thought the whole way through: *god is very near and hard to hold.*

Now she is covered in glue and bits of paper, the feral night still ringing inside her. The other children call her Moaning Maria, after a character from some popular film for children, which she has not seen. But she has never moaned! Not once has she moaned. The children around her play a slapping game and, just above this *slap slap* sound, she listens to the complex arithmetic of the bugs in her skull, intricate black clicking spirals. When she was a baby, she'd assumed that everyone had these bugs in their skulls. But soon enough it became apparent she was alone. *apples on a stick just make me sick   make my tummy go two-forty-six   not because I'm dirty   not because I'm clean   just because I kissed a boy behind a magazine*

106

"Maria?" Toby says from the seat behind her, "How is your mother?"

Toby too is incapable of belonging to any of this. Though in his case it results from his not having control over his own soul, and so messing his pants each evening in Social Studies. Maria simply hasn't control over her mind. And that is nothing to fear and in any case she hates it when people force her to think about her mother.

She turns around in the seat and stands on her knees, to face him. "Entropy, Toby, is the supreme force, presides over all others, will survive all others.—And yours?" He writhes under her gaze, as usual. For this, secretly, she loves him. She turns back around without waiting for his response.

Awful summer sunlight pours in through the windows and onto the large blue carpet of the classroom. Each child sits upon this carpet now, waiting to be read a story about a spider who makes a friend. Maria likes the spider very much, but she does not understand how he associates with that moronic cardinal, Randy. All he does is blabber about bliss. Some things really do not need our insistent praise.

Later, Maria gives her presentation on the evolution of the eye. It goes just as she had planned except that, at the end, one of the other children asks her this question:

"How come is it that when the lights go out I get scared? If everyone starts out with no eyes?"

Maria thinks about this a moment. The teacher watches anxiously. Finally Maria explains. "To be given a gift is to be given a cruelty, because a gift is a promise of its own revocation."

The teacher gives her a B.

✳

To underscore the madness of this place they call the world, Maria's older brother, Gerard, is the ice-cream truck driver. He lives down the road. Every morning the ice-cream truck sits out on the street, waiting to wail and chatter through the neighborhood. She passes it on her way to school, on her way home. She watches as the snow covers it all winter, piling high atop the giant fiberglass ice-cream cone, then melting away.

In the summers, Maria can hear his truck whinnying all throughout town. Sometimes, late at night, she knocks on his door and asks to go riding in it. Gerard always says yes. It is his greatest virtue.

Today Maria sits with Gerard on his back porch. A dark cat stands before them, mutilating a chipmunk. The cat claws carelessly at the little body, and the little body twitches helplessly.

"Whose cat is this?" Gerard asks. He has trouble speaking because he is eating a sandwich. He and Maria both are.

"It's Mrs. Bobbitt's."

The cat stares down at the chipmunk with wide eyes, as though unable to believe its lively desperation.

"He was born to kill," Gerard says.

Maria smiles. Most of the bugs lie sleeping quietly in her head now. There is only the gentle purr of fruit-flies. "This cat," she replies calmly, "and the world."

Gerard looks at her. "That cat's almost as warped as you are, Little Nothing." Maria giggles uncontrollably. Little Nothing! She *loves* when he calls her that. Some of the sandwich falls out of her mouth as she laughs. "You haven't hardly learned how to operate that body of yours and already you're set on leaving it?"

Maria shifts and, with a loose wrist, lifts the sandwich into the air, as though it were a wine glass. "Necessary precautions must be made. It is not we that leave the world, but the world that leaves us."

"Yeah well, just finish your sandwich." The sandwich is peanut butter and banana, and it is quite good.

※

Gerard has a secret. He does something that no one knows about except for Maria. He writes poetry.

It is late evening and the sky is like a bowl of melting sherbet. "What do you think about this one?" he asks, and reads her a poem he has just written.

"Hmm," Maria says, afterward. "You may be onto something. But you're still trying to please other people, Gerard."

Gerard does not understand. "Who would I be trying to please with this?" But Maria does not answer him. She has her own travails to sort out. The bugs have awoken again, and tonight they are like fireworks, blossoming ceaselessly from an unknowable center. Gerard fiddles with enjambment, placing the pencil in his mouth when not in use.

"I have to go finish something," Maria says. She has been absently tearing leaves apart for the last fifteen minutes. "Let's go on a drive later," she says.

※

In her bedroom, she paints the sculpture a series of gray tones. A great proud tragedy, as is every attempt to create. She will name the sculpture Beëlzebub, after Satan's cowardly assistant, and she will place him in the hallways of her school; for her imagination, with regards to the physical, is unfortunately stunted, due to such circumstances as are out of her control. No matter, Beëlzebub will stand there in the hallways of Greenly Elementary for many hours, perhaps even all day long. At least until they find a dolly to haul him away, as he is filled with concrete, and not easily lifted. Until then everyone will have to walk beneath him and his long pitiful arms. Beëlzebub, sweet Lord of the Flies. Eight feet tall, but meant to reach much higher, his sadness will rain onto everything—mandatory, prescribed, out of their hands.

Around midnight, the bugs calm themselves, the frantic ticking subsides into a cool rupturing sound. Flies play together in the sticky blood which no doubt pools inside her. She knocks on Gerard's front door. He opens it. Just behind Maria, Beëlzebub is lying in her father's green wheelbarrow, staring at the sky through his black lumpy eyes.

"I need some help," Maria says.

✳

The night is a wide black burn and both of them love it. The truck cries. That is what it does. There is no other word for it. The truck cries through the streets.

"What are all these people doing out at this hour?" Gerard asks. "Why are they dressed like that?"

Beëlzebub smiles sadly from the back of the ice-cream truck, occasionally hitting his head when they cut a sharp turn.

"It looks like Halloween," Maria says. Yes, it's obvious now. Tonight is Halloween, and neither of them knew it. "Christ on a cracker," Maria says, "are these my... *colleagues?*... You need to get us out of here, now."

"I'm going as fast as I can. What, you want me to hit one of these little monsters and get my ice-cream license revoked?"

"Well, it would be in harmony with the forces of this universe. Though to say I *want* it may perhaps be too much." Rows of children, in a garb once reserved for occult lunacy, wander dumbly through the streets in search of Snickers. Many of them insist upon breathing, though snot-bubbles build up in their noses and obstruct the effort.

"Pandemonium..." Maria mutters.

Maria knows which door the janitors leave unlocked. She has wandered toward this building many times at night. Gerard helps her haul Beëlzebub into the building and place him in the foyer of the Fourth Grade wing. When at last he looms at an angle that satisfies her, they step back to look at him. He stands in the dark, casting a long brittle shadow down the hall, afraid to be left alone.

Maria says to him "Fear is the essence of cruelty, my little monster," and they go back out to the truck.

"Listen," Gerard says, "I wrote a really good one earlier tonight. You want to hear it?"

"Yes," she says. He always asks, though she always wants to hear.

"Okay," he says.

After he reads, Maria takes the piece of paper from his hand and inspects it. She reads over the poem again. "You misspelled *awful*," she says.

"Yeah, I always spell that word wrong. But I kind of like it."

"I really like it."

Gerard looks at her. "You like the poem?"

"No," she says simply, "the misspelling. I really like it. You did a good thing."

✻

The bugs inside are sometimes so kind, as when the light comes back in rainbows from the million phosphorescent fly eyes, or when the candy-black wasps construct their papery chapels. At times, the morning sun rests over these things as gently as a blanket. At times, the brain of each insect is replaced by a tuft of fog.

Maria does not attend school today. Why should she have to walk beneath her own sadness? Already she does this every hour. Instead, she and Gerard ride the ice-cream truck down I-20. Sometimes she stands behind the driver's seat, and places her hands over Gerard's eyes.

"Stop doing that!" he yells. But anger toward Maria always melts away. He cannot understand it. It must be the reason he loves her so.

They eat lunch at a place called Ready or Not, which mostly sells cheeseburgers to the very unwell.

"Do you think Beetlebub is making lots of friends on his first day at school?" Gerard asks.

"Probably they've already stuffed him into an incinerator," Maria says. "God willing."

"Oh no. No, I was just starting to like him. He had such pretty eyes. Like an alligator's."

"Beauty is simply power, Gerard, and power is simply a fire waiting to end."

"I think you read too much.—Hey, you want to hear the poem I wrote this morning? It's about your sculpture."

"Mmm-hmm."

"Okay. You ready?"

"Mmm-hmm."

"Okay. Are you sure?"

"Yes!"

"Alright! Here it is..."

Ready or Not rests just at the edge of the highway, where civilization is stemmed by the desert. Several vultures circle a dumpster full of what can barely be called cow. Maria thinks of the children, of their stepping one after another beneath Beëlzebub's bent frame, some no doubt looking up into his savagely sorry eyes, still wet with paint, and feeling a loss, an inexplicable loss of something that never quite was. She would like for them to know what true loss feels like. Just for a moment. To know the pain of a thing that's never been.

"Well?" her brother asks eagerly.

"It's not bad," she confesses.

II

The little girl watches a boxing match. It is Saturday. The fever-ish flapping of monarch butterflies and tiger moths floods her head. Each time one boxer strikes another, the insects surge and sing like a brilliant, crêpey fire. When her father is away—and he is often—she goes into his office to find footage of old fights on the internet. She cannot help it; these boxers seem to rise up from someplace other. Her favorite fighter so embodies terror that she has placed a poster of him on her bedroom wall. In particular, she likes the swiftness with which he ruins the careers of the men he strikes, and the unnerving smile he wears afterward.

Once, he promised an opponent that even his name would be broken. Once, he told a man that God would devour his smile, that this was a divine birthright. Once, at a press conference, he leapt from a table and onto a jeering fan who had said something petty to him. Another time, a reporter asked him what it felt like to be Champion of the World. The boxer replied, *I don't know nothin about champion. I'm not champion of nothin. I'm just a boy that got aten by the world and made into a devil.*

Often Maria lies in bed staring up at the poster. It depicts the boxer baring his teeth at the sky, his sweat luminescent beneath the stadium lights, which cast long shadows over his face, leaving just darkness where the eyes should be. Blood runs from his face down his neck in vibrant red rivulets. Though this—the blood—is surely someone else's.

On mute, she watches the boxer end another's spirit. She hums Rachmaninoff's First, kicking her legs back and forth in the spinny chair. This fight occurred far away, in Atlantic City, many years before she was born. The boxer has long since retired and, as though in a grand finale, gone on to destroy even himself.

Ruckus lies in his favorite corner, violently chewing at a section of his side until it is as pink and as glistening as the guts of a grapefruit. He looks up. He thinks, *Something is off...*

The black snow of Rachmaninoff falls from Maria's mouth: "Hmm hmm, hmm hmm, hmm hmm!" The phone rings. Toby.

"Hi Maria," he says.

"Toby."

"I was just calling to make sure you're okay. You didn't come to school yesterday."

"Yes well," Maria says, spinning in the spinny chair, "order is an illusion."

"Okay. But are you okay? How's your mother?"

Maria stares up at the ceiling; a coffee-colored watermark has sprawled itself out overtime. "Toby. I have to go now." Already the fight is over. The boxer has put his opponent down early in the second round, is lifted now into the air by a group of men in red silk robes, men from his corner. He grins, floating above the crowd, but his eyes say something other. DEATH, they say, DEATH. Maria hangs up the phone, goes to ride her bike around the neighborhood a while.

❊

The weekend is a wicked box of sun. Light weeps across the land. She sits in the graveyard consuming a peach. The spiders stitch a veil inside her head, their thousand hungry legs clicking together. When they breathe they breathe in unison, so that the sound becomes perceptible: a noise like someone wincing. Maria draws quick black sketches, violent and tangled. She would like to find her next creation, but it will not come. She thinks of her dream again, the one she had last night. She'd received a letter from Rodin—written on fine crimson silk—in which he confessed his affections to her and begged her to come stay in Paris with him. *I am unconcerned as yet with the suffering life of flesh*, she wrote back, *sorry*.

This had been a nightmare.

Light withers by eight each evening and in this Maria thrives; all her bones scream to be loosed of mass. The Gift of Desperation, Gerard called this feeling once, a phrase he had learned in A.A. But Maria's drawings are nothing if not able to lift her up from this life, and today they are nothing.

There is Angel in Descent, to be fashioned out of 12-gauge copper wire, but it is nothing. Magdalena, out of plaster, like-wise nothing. Bach on Deathbed, made from draped white linen. Nothing. A petty trick. There is the Boiled Child, and there is the Hushing, and there is a Secret Rain.

None reveals itself to be the delicate portal she seeks.

A murder of crows sweeps down, engulfs a ruined maple. They speak some hot black secret which a hundred years ago could still be heard. The town has long been troubled by these birds, by their vicious shrieking. A year ago the city council passed an ordinance to have them all removed. Men came in big white trucks with cages in the backs and tried to lure the crows into them. The city spent 1.2 million dollars on this project, but it did not work. The crows are happy as ever, screaming and beating their wet black wings.

Maria pulls from her backpack a length of Italian bread, which she purchased from a sub shop in anticipation of these crows. She tears pieces off and throws them. The birds totter toward her.

"Hello little angels," she says, "What message do you have for me today?" They gaze at her maniacally through their wide black eyes, waiting for more. "I should like to tell you a secret which crows have never heard," she says, "but in exchange you first must tell me some crow secrets." The birds peck fiercely at one another, bickering over bits of bread as they land. More crows drift down from the sky like cinders from a fire. There are almost two-dozen of them now. When all the hunks have been devoured they gather at her feet and stare. "What's that?" she asks coyly.

HA HA, the crows answer. *HA HA. HA HA.* Pale sunlight fills their open mouths. Maria crumples up the empty bread bag. "The Lenape Indians..." she begins, " believed that a rainbow crow brought fire to earth. A burning stick. He carried it in his mouth, all the way from heaven. It took him three days." HA, the crows repeat. *HA. HA HA.* "Shhh! Let me finish! On the first day, the fire burned his tail. On the second day, the soot blackened his feathers. And on the third day, the stick had grown so short that the smoke filled his mouth and made him hoarse." *HA HA,* say the crows. *HA HA. HA HA. HA HA.* Grim chaos made of nothing. *HA HA.* Spinning waters which choke the sink. *HA. HA.* Maria listens closely. HA. She has only just begun to discern their meaning when the dark pool of bodies bubbles and bursts and fills the sky like a smoke-bomb. It is the groundskeeper, who startles them away, pulling up in his raspy golf-cart.

"Little girl," he says. "Why don't you go on out of here and do Little Girl things and leave the dead alone." Maria closes her notebook, places it in her bag, and stares at him. He looks like a skeleton in a baseball cap. "Go on!" he says. "Why don't you go on and play? Go on and be like the others. You'll get to have your stay here before long." She stares at the shingly surface of his face, terrified. The empty bread bag unfurls beside her. "Go on!" he says again, and waves her away.

✳

It is dark when Maria returns home, but this is only a reprieve. The sun will return tomorrow. And again the next day. It will seem to go on like this forever. But Maria knows that the sun only has five billion years until it burns out—not even a blip in the span of things—and by then it will have already swollen up and absorbed the adjacent planets. Something to look forward to.

At first she can not see him in the dark, but there is Toby, sitting on the front steps of her house. "Toby—"

"Maria I'm sorry to be such a weirdo, I was just really worried about you, and you didn't come to school yesterday. How is your mother?"

"Toby," Maria says, "are you much familiar with physics?" She steps toward him and he seems to flinch. Gnats now, behind her eyes. So many gnats she can hardly see.

"No..." he says, and looks down at his lap. In his hand are pitiful flowers, a wilted clutch of dandelions. He has not even yet learned his times tables.

"Well Toby," she begins, "in physics..." but the heavy cloud of gnats flits over her thinking and drowns it, so that she has to stop a moment and collect herself. Toby looks up with concern, as though she needs something from him. She begins again. "In physics they say that, with intensity, a drop evaporates. By law." The whooshing of gnats has become a great gray fire, filling her with its roar. At present Toby is saying something about the dog, about Ruckus, but it is difficult to hear him over the thundering gnats. He seems to speak of the peculiar lumps which populate the dog's neck and spine, as though worry will dissolve them. Ruckus lies in the yard, in a patch of dirt he has worn into the lawn over the years. He is happy to be included.

Maria begins to walk past Toby, but he rises and gets in the way. He is holding out his sickly flowers. "I just don't want you to think you're invisible," Toby tells her. She thinks of her boxer, of his exquisite black movements around the ring, of his agile arms which douse the self. She steps toward Toby. She thinks of striking him—and then she does.

When this happens, she can feel the tissues of his muscle collapse under the force. Now, there is real red blood peeking out from Toby's lip. They gaze at one another in terror. His eyes well up and she expects him to run away, but he stands there, staring at her. The dog lifts itself and lets out a worthless bark, then another. He watches them carefully, his tail swinging low. When, after some time, they do not move, he goes back to his dirt and lies down, exhausted.

"Oh," Maria says, and touches her own lip in the place where Toby's has split. "Does it need ice?" All the bugs have flown away for now. Toby does not answer her. Still, she takes him by the hand and leads him into the kitchen.

In the light of the house, his cut does not look so bad, though his face is flush and glittering with tears. "You want a freezy-pop?"

she asks, rifling through the freezer. She emerges holding two. "Red or blue?" she asks. Toby does not speak but, cautiously, he takes the blue one. They sit at the kitchen table. The only sound is of an old clock on the wall. It is a cuckoo clock, but the mechanism has failed. The wooden bird has not been seen in years.

"Did you know," Maria says, "that crows can recognize subtleties in human facial expressions? As a survival mechanism. They can tell when we're experiencing anger, and when we're experiencing joy, and—"

Toby scoots his chair back suddenly. Then he gets up, and leaves. The blue popsicle sits on the table, melting in front of Maria. Now that he has gone, she expects to feel relief but, for some reason, she cannot.

✳

That night she is a spindly woolen spider, wandering through the hallways of her school. The spider sits in class, its legs bunched up behind its desk. Around the spider sit the children, absorbed in what the teacher says. The teacher hands the spider back a test, though instead of a letter grade, there is a brown burn; each page has been eaten through by fire. It tries to get up, to go to the restroom, but it cannot extricate its many legs from the desk, they are tangled. It struggles, but all the bristling legs are knotted together. The teacher comes over and, using a tissue, smushes the spider, and throws the wad away.

Hot ash sails through Sunday. The local library, finally, has achieved its great desire, has built in itself a cathedral of burning. God's spine drips down though a stalk of black smoke and ends at the tip of this fire. Maria stands behind a crowd, watching the blithe demise of the building. She observes with great fascination. It seems just that all those words should break, that the sky should bear them away.

Maria steps forward, until the heat of the flames is faintly felt. She thinks of the dark insides of the crystal cave which her class took a trip to last year. When the guide aimed her flashlight at the cavern walls, a glittering devoured the eye. Otherwise, simple emptiness resolved the space. How mighty and endless the end is.

A woman in form-fitting jogging clothes stands at the front of the crowd. "This is a catastrophe!" she says. Maria turns to the woman.

Thin white wires lead down from her head to a phone, fastened at the forearm.

"You're going to be very surprised about death," Maria

informs the woman. "That much is clear." The lungs of the day choke brilliant and black.

"Excuse me?" The woman says, but Maria does not feel it necessary to excuse her. There is no excuse for cowardice. "Young lady," the woman says, but Maria does not remove her gaze from the inferno. Just behind the ears, mosquitos fly in twisted pairs, dancing to the song of new blood through the veins.

The firefighters stand together beside their red truck. They have decided that the best course is to let the fire burn itself out. They watch too, the library moaning before them. They watch and they argue, vehemently, over what to make for dinner.

Maria continues her descent into town. She goes to the hardware store, to buy supplies. Her father gives her money for meals each month, but she eats little. Instead, she needs paint: benevolent black and relentless white and fat fat red. She needs nails. She needs a new brush, a bag of plaster mix, a two-inch chisel, several yards of chain. This, she believes, will be enough. There are only so many things one person may need.

When she approaches the register, the man behind the counter is soldering something intricate, something so small he needs a heavy magnifying glass just to see it.

"Hello Maria," he says, and ceases his work. "I see you got big plans today."

"I'm going to build a portal out of being," she tells him.

The man laughs. He smokes a cigarette. The law does not matter to him. He pulls in a lungful, and he laughs a great deal, the ribbon of smoke drawing up from his hand. Then he says, "Gonna need some rebar, aren't ya?" It is true. The needs are never-ending. She goes and comes back with five lengths of rebar. While the man calculates her total, Maria looks at the small object he has been soldering. It is silver, about the size of a cigarette butt.

"What is that?" Maria asks, peering at the thing. In the shifting light it seems to shiver.

"This? This is one of my angels," the man says. "Her name is Sylvia."

Maria looks more closely at the angel. It is hard to discern any details in it. Strands of silver stray from it like hairs. She looks at the man again, though periodically she glances back to the angel suspiciously. "What is it for?" she asks.

"For? Not a thing. I just like angels." The man's smile is so bright one must avert their gaze. "You know," he says, "what the best way to sort out being is?" Maria looks at the silver cigarette again. It seems that if she touched one of the metal hairs, it would prick her and draw blood. "Not exiting, Maria. No. You just gotta slow down, way way down, until time is so stretched out that you can rest in the space between seconds." The man gives her her change, and returns to his work, smoke unfurling from the soldering gun, from the lit cigarette. Light plays brightly off of his glasses. "I used to be in a hurry," he says. "But it'll take more time than I got, building enough angels to make a heaven." The gun snaps and pops suddenly. "And the angels don't like to be rushed," he says quietly, looking down at the clot of silver. "Do you sweetheart?"

There are many scars winding up and down the man's arm, white as water vapor. He no longer looks at Maria. Instead, he sings, peering dreamily through the magnifying glass, working.

"Nice to see you again," he says, as Maria exits the store. "Come back again."

❦

Her backpack is heavy with materials but it is important she carry this weight, if she is ever to arrive. She cannot stay in her house long. The work must be done elsewhere. She will only sketch the plans here. From her mother's room comes the violent sound of television: an audience laughing endlessly, emptying themselves into each other over and over until nothing is left but their cacophonous attrition. Maria shuts her bedroom door and begins to draw up her portal. The paper she uses, large and translucent, is intended for a doctor's exam table, and unspools from a heavy roll. Over the top of her plan she writes SOME ARE BORN TO SWEET DELIGHT SOME ARE BORN TO ENDLESS NIGHT. The walls of this house rattle and whisper and drop back down into the earth at a considerable rate.

Arrival is no place. The journey comes to be its own country. If Maria is ever to learn this, she will need to keep moving. She finishes her plan, stands over it, smiling, the heat of the ink lifting off of the page. She rolls the paper up, packs the materials into her bag, and leaves. On her way out, the phone is ringing, but she must maintain momentum. She can almost hear, calling out from the other room, a voice, frail and thirsting. But this must be mere chimera.

Maria builds her gateway in the graveyard. This, the only place where silence reigns, and requests fall away. The bag reads PLAS-TER OF PARIS, and the material is dense and difficult to mix. She slaps handfuls of it against the ground, many times, until a threshold can be deciphered. One heavy rebar rod she stakes in on either side. The skull fills with a glamourous tide of milk-white larvae, freshly spawned. Like a sea of ivory tongues, they blindly writhe and wander over one another. They want, without knowing what. It is everywhere in nature just this way.

Maria gazes up at the sky where the moon hangs at midday, due to simple spatial circumstance. She packs the plaster against the rebar spines and lets it ooze down to the earth. She packs it again. The plaster covers her to the wrists and dries into a spectral, chalky hull, which cracks away when a fist is made. A life of this could easily be spent. When the posts have been built out enough to satisfy her, she stakes more rebar atop them and continues on, though they stand at desperate slants now. When the plaster dries it is still fixed in its rutted, dripping form. In the head the slick larvae form a white mire into which everything else falls. A sound just like a swimming pool sucks against the borders of the brain.

Across the two beams Maria balances another length of rebar horizontally, which she packs into place to create a header. More material is tamped over top of it. She stands inside the new opening. It is no larger than a closet door. As she works, the plaster rains down on her like heavy snow and dries in opaque icicles. Maria continues to pack clods of plaster onto the portal until she runs out. When she has finished, she stands inside the frame, neither entering nor exiting, merely examining the jagged white layers that surround her. Her eyes are watering, though she cannot say why. It simply happens that way sometimes.

※

Strange, but the world keeps on. Maria sits on a high barstool in Gerard's kitchen. He is making Belgian waffles and intermittently rubbing his temples. Maria kicks her legs back and forth, watching impassively. Lice like a thin mist fall down through the dark night of the mind. Some fall into the seams between thought and nestle there. Whenever densely gathered, the lice bear a creamy color. Gerard has had a hard day. Sundays are always difficult for him. More children than one would ever hope to see. From atop the fridge, Saint-Saëns gallops along on a compact disc.

"Animals," Gerard says, "all those kids are lawless furless animals."

"Though animals can keep themselves alive," Maria says.

"Talk to them for me, would you?"

"I don't, typically..."

"Just tell them I'm tired. Tell them I'm out of strawberry."

"I don't suspect they'd understand," she says. "They've yet to develop such regard for the entropic." The waffle batter claps and hisses from inside the iron.

"Well I just don't understand how so many can come to one place. Hordes."

Maria thinks of the terracotta army, stationed for the last twenty-two hundred years in the Lintong District. The 8,000 clay soldiers were commissioned by the emperor Qin sometime after his thirteenth birthday. He had them placed underground, to guard his soul following his death, but in the 1970s someone uncovered them and promptly built a museum on top of the site.

"Oftentimes," Maria says, "we are more our own determinants than we know."

Gerard pitches the waffle out of the iron and onto a stack of others just like it. He pours more batter into the iron. His efforts are unceasing, though neither he nor Maria much like waffles. "You're right. I should never have quit my job at Luella's."

"That's not particularly what I meant," Maria says. Before being an ice-cream truck driver, Gerard had been a bouncer at a bar called Luella's, a place where—as far as Maria could tell—people came to pursue the inane whims of certain biological imperatives.

"You want a waffle or no?"

"Okay."

In the den Maria and Gerard sit eating their waffles. They watch several potted plants huddled together on the coffee table; there is no television. The colocasia and the pencil plant and the fiddle-leaf fig and the aloe vera and the begonia all together huddle, conferring in hushed tones.

Gerard eats nine waffles, stacked one on top of the next, with a pat of butter for each. "You're acting funny today," he says. It is true that the self is a wandering state. Maria stares at her empty plate, having finished her waffles. With a single tine of her fork, she sketches wild spirals in the ochre-colored syrup on the plate.

"I had a bad dream last night," she says. "But I feel better now."

"Hmm..." Gerard says, "You want some more?"

"Okay."

Gerard takes the plates into the kitchen and Maria sits watching the plants. They only appear to be still. In truth they move almost as fast as her, stretching themselves upward, waiting to break under the weight of their own height. "Shh!" she says to them. "You're being too loud!"

Gerard comes back in with another half-dozen waffles on each plate. "When I was little," he says, "I used to have this dream that I was being babysat by this old man. He wore a suit and he never spoke, and I knew he was me at a later age." He hands Maria her plate. "What was your dream about?"

"A test," she says, and takes another bite of belgian waffle.

"I don't know what I ever had against these things," Gerard says, staring with wonder at his food. "Who came up with this?" There is one plant separate from the rest—an asparagus fern seated in the corner—who gazes out murderously at everyone else in the room. "They're sinful."

"Kafka felt that impatience was the sin from which all others are derived."

"Well he also wrote nightmares as a hobby," Gerard says, as though settling the matter.

Maria looks up at him. "You're in a bad mood," she says.

He stands up and takes her plate, still with half a waffle on it. "Behind the world our names enclose," he says, "is the nameless."

"Who is that?"

"What makes you think it's not me?"

"Who?"

"It's Rilke," Gerard tells her, and stomps away indignantly.

✻

It is a cold light that fireflies produce, even in the gnashing pink blush of the brain. As Maria lies in bed they fire off at nothing in particular. Staring at the ceiling, she waits for sleep. She hates this, this waiting. In the skull the bugs blink in syncopated torpor. Blink.   Blink.   The whole head, flickering like a shard-scattered lawn.

Suffering stops with the sufferer. Maria must learn this. She waits for sleep and it waits for her too.

IV

Sick sad slashes of sun tear through Maria's bedroom. All night she has dreamed of unbearable steam, beating her skin from within. The steam escaped through several openings: the lips, the nose, the navel, each of the delicate eye-sockets. It screamed out from her fingernails, blew open every tip of her and hissed away. The heat of this steam had seemed enough to die from. But she had not died; only boiled and wailed and wept, the way the dying do. The fruits of this—before waking—were no more than the meager tatters of her person.

Now she sits in bed and waits for her alarm to sound. It is not yet morning, though the night is through. She looks to Ruckus, who lies whimpering against the wall, still sleeping. In his dream, he stands in the corner and cowers. For there is someone cruel and tall, lying there in the bed beside Maria. He barks and barks but they do not move. They merely lie and face the ceiling. With a furious fear he watches them and growls. Each breath he takes expands the room, collapses it. He wakes, thin film over his eyes, and gazes shyly at Maria, still stunned by the light of this bright otherworld. *Hungry*, he thinks, and wanders from the room.

Outside, the day deforms the night again. No one else has woken. Bugs beat themselves to pieces against the hot porchlight inside her. Fragments of their wings like black confetti cling to nearby cobwebs. Maria will forgo the bus today, enter the hungry eave of the town by foot. Rain the night before has left behind a mirror of the world and everywhere Maria steps it soaks her to the socks. Light crowds the sky, worth no more than the dark it devours.

Halfway to school, she is set upon by the groundskeeper, who stands at the border of his graveyard, as though he has been waiting for her there all night.

"I see you think of this as a Little Girl playground huh," he says, "You think here you can make all your wild messes and the dead won't care? Well, you're wrong Little Girl." He smiles, a wild, metallic smile. Over one eye rests a swollen violet gash, from which rainwater drips. "I guess you think I like to clean all that white shit up? All day long! Soon as the rain hit your little sand castle it melted and it run into Ms. Aberdeen's plot and I'm the one had to scoop it all out." Maria has stopped walking. She cannot possibly proceed. "I guess you think it'll all just wash away clean, but oh Little Girl how wrong you are." He holds a length of the rebar. "I'm the one has to clean it all up," he says. In his hand the steel, still dusted white with plaster, seems like a monstrous orchestral baton. He waves it overhead as he speaks. "All day long I clean and think, who would be so careless and irreverent over top the dead? Who would be so silly and so little and slick as to decide to make messes wherever the dead lay? Who? And you know I could only think of one Little Girl." He steps toward her. It seems something has shattered in his gaze overnight. Maria steps back, the bumblebees inside prepared to sting themselves away. "What you got to say about yourself?" he asks. "What?" Maria cannot speak. He watches her a moment and, still holding the rebar overhead, he closes his eyes.

All at once Maria feels the cold damp feet beneath her. She

hears—as soft and indeterminate as the dust of a butterfly—a voice, which rings from the space just behind her.

surrender, it says. She wants to turn around and look; she wants to see the source of it. *surrender*, it says again. She keeps her gaze ahead, fixed on the groundskeeper, but her mind has turned back, twisted itself so to better hear the voice. She cannot— having strained herself— hear the sound any clearer, though still she is happier trying in this way.

At last she closes her eyes. She closes her eyes and she sees a man in The Inferno, there in the final chasm, a man with his torso torn long by Dante, both hands spreading wide his chest. She holds her eyes closed and she waits. The man mutters to himself. *oh hard earth,* he asks, *why didn't you open then?* Each organ drops down from the hole he holds open. *perché non t'apristi?*

When Maria hears crying, she opens her eyes again. The groundskeeper has bent himself toward the ground, as though he has been struck, and he sobs into one hand.

But still Maria cannot walk through this, it is a thing she cannot pass. He keeps his eyes low. "Helen," he says into his hand, almost too quiet to hear, whimpering. "Oh Helen," he says.

Now, Maria turns and runs—as fast as she can—in the wrong direction. She will run until she cannot breathe, and all along the way bright light will bear down overhead.

❋

Last summer Maria's father had taken her on a trip to the Grand Canyon. This had been strange for them both. The lost may only ever touch the lost, it seems. The canyons had been a great tower of vacancy, and could affect no change in either of them. But, on the way back, they stopped at an art museum. A shattered

Renaissance sculpture had just been restored after fifteen years of careful planning. What the museum had done was glue the sculpture back together, using specially designed harnesses to hold each piece in place. The sculptor's name had been Tullio Lombardo. Tullio's father had been among the greatest sculptors of the 15th century. On Tullio's deathbed, he asked for a wooden headstone. 'I am tired of looking at marble,' is how he put it.

The museum was very proud of what they had done. They erected a special exhibit, explaining in detail how the sculpture had been restored. It had been shattered into 138 pieces, and now it looked almost as though nothing had happened. 'Adam,' is what Tullio named the thing.

"Something so broken should just be thrown away," Maria's father said on the ride home, and she could not contest this.

꙳

A flood has filled her head somehow, left the ants to crawl skull walls in panicked droves, each following the other's winding path. They reach the top, where there is nothing for them, and begin their descent back down. Maria goes to Gerard's house, but he is not home. She stands outside her own house, looking in from the street. She feels she is merely some stranger who, walking by, has stopped for a moment to stare. A faint sound comes from inside: a kind of mew. Soon, she will have to go in there. But not yet.

The light pours in from even the tenderest angle. Maria takes the long way to school, follows the town's crumbling edges, rather than enter its center. By the time she has arrived she is several hours late. Everyone has gone to recess, leaving the classroom empty. Maria sits down on the carpet, looks at the clock, waits.

The carpet is stiff and blue and synthetic, disclosing, Maria feels, the trajectory of things. She sits and she waits. The service this carpet has provided to the class, thus far, is as a venue for story-time. Every Monday and Thursday they listen to stories, though Maria has missed today's session. When her class returns from recess, they will find her there on the carpet, and then they will want to know where she has been. But that will not be possible.

UNFISHED,
UNFINISHED

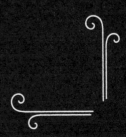

unfinished

ars poetica

"unfinished"
(ars poetica)

What I want most is to go
or else savor each stroke.
but the truth is I keep thinking about how this comic will end
...whether or not you like the lines, the words...
if it makes sense,
if it's too stiff...
so that I end up not really present in what I'm doing.
and then it isn't very fun for either of us.

but there are ways to wrench myself free...
allow myself surprises.
To be honest...
I'm not quite sure how it works.
In fact, the less I under-stand, the better.
but I'd like to try to talk with you about it anyway...

For example, I've made all these notes and practice strokes. Like this:

It's not the same as being careless.

But I'd like to try to e...

It definitely involves not being scared...

Being patient

But something i'd like to try to with a about an u

In fact, the less understand, the b

to ones... i'm quite sure how it works...

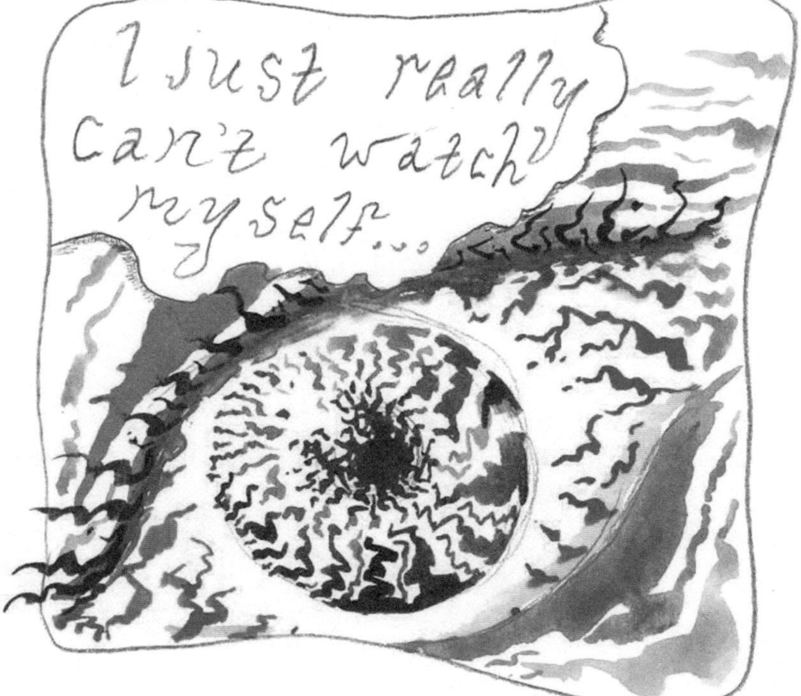
I just really can't watch myself...

A WHOLE NOTHER
WORLD

The animal began to rescue itself from the trash. Its name was Sunset, and it bore all the common markings of decay, save for the spiritual variety. Everyone had been looking for Sunset. For six weeks they had searched. When at last they found Sunset, they put it in the trash. 'Animal,' is not the word they would have used. They would have used the word 'trash.' But they did not need words, then. When one finds a piece of trash in hand, one wordlessly disposes of it.

Sunset crawled out from beneath the glistening black bags as though up from some dark flame. Sunset thought, *That was some bullshit. If ever I happen to see those mother fuckers again... well, I don't even know what I'll do.* Sunset thought many other thoughts besides, but all arrived at a similar terminus. For what, after all, *can* one do, under such profound constraints? With astonishing grace, Sunset vaulted over the lip of the dumpster and out into the sunshine.

My God, Sunset thought, and thought again, *My God. I'm so glad that spring is back.* Sunset licked at its paws for a time, and then coughed. Limping out into the street, Sunset began at once to feel, at the sight of the cars rushing by, an irrepressible urge for nicotine, which flooded its furry little body and rang like a bell. Sunset began walking without any notion of arrival. The city around it gnashed its teeth and sweated anxiously. When people saw Sunset walking toward them, they mostly crossed the street. Those who did not appeared to ready themselves for combat.

The night before, Sunset had been dreaming of its mother, who was long ago struck dead by a van. In the dream, she spoke very softly to Sunset, stroking its fine fur and giving it, sometimes, a light tickling. You are my tender little something, she had said. You are my precious little world. Just as she had when Sunset was a little one, she spoke these in the dream.

Sunset wiped something from its eye and, noticing a man outside of a bar who seemed unbothered by the sight of Sunset, stopped and asked to bum a smoke. The man eyed Sunset without turning toward it. "Depends," he said. "You okay with non-filtered?"

"Jesus Christ," Sunset said. "Yes." Sunset took the cigarette into its snout without yet having lit it and seemed, for just a moment, to be able to breathe unrestrained. The man reached out and lit it. Some sort of aria coursed out from the fire, down through the barrel of the cigarette, and into Sunset's worried breast. "Thanks," Sunset said. "I'd give you a quarter if I had one." The man nodded, looking out at a plastic bottle that sat in the street. Each time a car passed over it, the bottle produced the same rhythmic sequence. Tickle-tick-tat, tickle-tick-tat. "My mamma used to tell us," Sunset said, almost too quietly to hear, "that it only looked like grownups pulled the smoke out from the cigarettes they smoked—that really it was the cigarettes pulled something out from *them*. Damned if she wasn't right, huh..."

"*Shit*," the man said gruffly. "My mamma, that bitch wasn't right about a damn thing her whole life..." After this exchange, Sunset did not speak again, and when the cigarette had been depleted Sunset merely nodded cordially and carried on its way.

"God grant me the courage," Sunset said, walking away, "to keep on living in this place." Sunset walked as one might through a smoky building, urgently and with its head down, anticipating that at any moment all the fell flames would creep in and swallow it.

Eventually Sunset arrived at a dry and yellowed public park, and this seemed as good a place as any to sit down. In the distance, children played on the blacktop, and the sound of their dribbling quieted Sunset's mind. It lay down a while and went to sleep.

Abruptly Sunset was awoken by the screaming of another animal. To look at this creature it was clear at once, as it always was, that this too had been regarded now as trash for some time. "Get the fuck off my bench you fucking fuck!" it barked. Intermittently it growled at Sunset. Once or twice it came forward, biting at the air between them before darting back again and out of reach.

"Lord have mercy," Sunset said. "Will you calm your crazy ass down?" It happened often that the parks became a kind of dumping grounds. The animals in this place, they had so much life inside of them, with no way whatsoever to live it, and this resulted in a rather morbid overload—an electrification—of everyone, of the entire space, and at all hours of the day. Sunset could see, waking up from its nap, that there would be no restful moments here.

"Shut up!" the animal barked. "You narc FBI spy! Shut up and give me back my bench before I... Before I... You don't even want to know."

This was correct. Sunset threw up its paws and carried itself, wearily, away again.

※

In the midday heat, Sunset's marbled coat shone brilliantly, dappled though it was with scabs and scars—the many moments of disaster that lay always draped upon its skin. *I gotta find a telephone*, it thought. *I gotta get a hold of Tiny.* For that was Sunset's sister's name, its sole surviving relative, and the hope that Tiny could afford to help it get a hotel room for the night seemed all the hope it had now. Sunset grew listless. It strolled uneasily against the sun. The bright beam of hunger burned its way up through Sunset's stomach, beginning somewhere deep within and crawling out, until it grasped the walls where Sunset walked. Sunset stumbled, rather desperately, into the first doorway that opened, out from the heat and into a cool cafe. The man at the counter watched Sunset intently as it approached him. The look on his face was simple, unmistakable. Anyone would know it. Hate, they sometimes call it. Hate. Sunset began to ask if there might be a phone that it could use. It struggled to remain calm as it communicated, though the hunger made this difficult. The man watched placidly as Sunset spoke. Sunset was too tired to dispel the man's cold feeling. It merely wished to reach someone familiar. It finished speaking and then waited.

The man smiled something mortifying. "Our phones are for the patrons," he said. He was possessed of upper-management dispassion. Because Sunset could feel something horrific was about to take place, it turned abruptly and walked away, the patrons eying at it wearily as it did so. The beam of hunger still screamed out, dragging its burning bright nails across the doorframe behind Sunset as it left, though no one else could see this.

Back on the street, things had grown worse. The world began to tilt and turn before Sunset, and the sky had grown a sickening gray. Through this Sunset went on, the pads of its paws already rubbed ragged by asphalt. The sky darkened still more overhead, and then roared, so that all the people standing in the streets—all those who had been watching through the day as Sunset passed them—disappeared into the many buildings that they owned. Then, the streets were cleared, and Sunset was alone left there to walk them. At last the sky split, and the downpour began. It was shame, what fell down, shame down onto Sunset. Shame, in great roaring sheets, as those indoors looked on. Shame, soaking through Sunset's ragged coat, and shame running over Sunset's face.

Sunset hurried away and into another building, if only to stop the downpour, for a moment. This was a library it had entered. An elderly woman stood at the front desk. She looked enough like Sunset's mother that, on first entering, Sunset began without comprehension to cry.

"Young man?" she said, and came out from behind the desk. "Young man," she said again. "What's the matter?" And then she touched his hand. He looked up at her. She was looking at him. "Baby," she said. "You just tell me what's the matter. We'll see what we can do, if you just tell me what it is." And, although Sunset so badly wished to, he was not sure how he might start.

MENTION OF FLESH

My 6-year-old told me my vagina has a tail. That's what she calls penises, vagina tails. Sometimes I'll be in the bathroom and Mercy—that's her name—she barges in. When this occurs, she looks up at me with disdain. I look at me too, for a minute.

Then I say, "Get *out*." But she goes on staring at me. At it. I say it again with more force, "get out!" And if she doesn't budge, I glare at her like, hello? Then the door snivels closed until there's only just a crack, some ringing border, watching me. Then it clicks completely.

This morning I watched my neighbor's house burn to the ground. Each timber collapsed into Earl's lawn. Earl stood there and watched. We all watched. Haggard cage of worried dust, what else could we do? Dollops of snow dropped and caught on the dry ground. The fire department came. I spoke with a fireman.

"Vagina tail?" the fireman asked. "No, my little Tad doesn't do that sort of weirdness."

"Oh," I said.

"My little guy does eat the debris beneath the couch cushions."

I was ready for him to move back to the fire, but, "Sometimes while sucking his thumb," the fireman went on, "he likes to gather a sizable booger ball on his upper lip and when I try to clean it off he yells, No! I want that! And he bites me on the darn hand." The firefighter chuckled. I watched the blaze lift behind him, rise up into the sky and kick the black house beneath it. The road was thick with spectators and I had errands to run, but the firefighter was still telling me about Tad. "Sometimes he slaps his stomach when he's happy. I asked him once why he does that. You know what he told me? He told me he's insane!" Then the firefighter flipped the lever on his nozzle and the long hose fattened and kicked behind him, sending a spew of water into the freezing day.

I didn't speak to Earl, who was crying alone on the curb.

"Mildred!" he screamed. "Mildred!" Which is his dog I think.

In the living room, Mercy gazes at *Mafia Bakers*. She's standing up on the couch, holding a popsicle. Sometimes she bounces. It's Saturday. *Mafia Bakers* is a reality tv show about incarcerated gangsters who've found peace in pastries. Right now Whitey Bulger, member of the infamous Patrarcia family, is making a torte. He's in an orange jumpsuit fashioned to look like a tux. Sometimes the guard approaches to zest a lemon, careful to hold the tiny serrates out of the mobster's reach. When the guard has zested enough, Whitey tells her to stop by saying calmly "Bada boom, my man."

"Is this the best thing on tv?" I ask.

"Can't you be like a fish and be quiet?" Mercy says, with her stupid little voice. Out the window, there's still the fire crackling. Earl is still fetal, all the yellow men in front of him buzzing through the lint of snow and soot. I walk toward Mercy and she catches me out of the corner of her eye, head still facing the tv screen. I pick up the remote.

"What else is on?" I say, with the warm, tender voice which I worked on with Dr. Phillips. Well, what else is on is: *Dixie Plastic Surgeon, Hip Hop Hoarders, United States of Truckers, This American Bro, It's Me Or The Moonshine, Most Eligible Fast Food Kings, Little Ghost People.* Also, *Extreme Exterminators: Ice T & Coco.* "What're they exterminating?" I ask, but I'm not really expecting an answer.

"Rats." Mercy says, matter-of-factly. Except she can't say her R's yet, so it's 'wats'.

I change the channel and end up with Whitey again. The camera pans over the prison guard, who is so thin, and young, maybe just twenty. She's got one hand on her zester, while the other grasps her belt, and she observes the baking with a certain wonder. The prisoner's hands are soft with flour. "I love Whitey," Mercy says, and falls into her seat. For a moment, the sirens outside drown everything out, so that I can't hear what the tv says, and I just watch Mercy, her eyes wide, I just watch her. It's so easy, she forgets I'm even here. Sirens wailing, but outside. I set the remote back down.

"I guess this is okay," I say, and glance out the window, where everyone is bleached with snow.

Yesterday at work: crackdown on graffiti. We painted the bathroom walls black. Me, standing on my knees, sleeves bundled up, black stains on my elbows, rolling the roller. Paunch Wheelis came in every fifteen minutes to check on me. Paunch is my higher-up. Said he didn't want the fumes to knock me out. Black stains on my palms. Paunch is tiny, but he wears a big pinstripe suit. I rolled the roller and looked at him.

I work for Tacos Tacos Tacos, in the corporate division. On a normal day, it's my job to come up with the phrases on the little hot sauce packets. It's important that they be raunchy, but not too raunchy. Also clever, but not too clever. Things like *I have but one squirt to give for my glory are a no go.* However, *When I grow up, I want to be a waterbed* has been a huge hit. But I also have other odd jobs around the office. When I'm feeling kind of poopie, I tell myself, this could be worse. I could still be working in the Dove Deodorant factory. I tell myself I'm doing this for Mercy.

"Okay, Mercy," I say, "time to do our drawing." Then together we move away from the television, into the dining room. Every morning I have my daughter sketch a self-portrait. It was Dr. Phillips's idea, but lately I'm not so sure. Lately she just draws her vagina, delicate crumpled linework, hung up on the fridge.

"I'm getting really sick of this, Monroe." Mercy says to me, because that's my name and that's okay.

"Well Dr. Phillips thinks it's a good idea," I say. Mercy wears a plastic sheriff's badge over the heart of her shirt.

"Well I hate Dr. Phillips," she says.

"No you don't," I say. "Mercy?" but she doesn't reply. "We're going on some errands today." She sits at the glass table, tilts her head, and draws. Around the corner, I can still see the tv burning with pigment. Mercy hums. She is a tangle of chaos on the page, swirling lumps of pink and copper, but her humming is sweet.

When she's finished, I lift her drawing, snap it onto the fridge with a magnet, and take a step back. An agonal knot of pastel colored pencil: my little girl.

"C'mon, sweet. Let's go," I say. I slump into the wall and wait for her to rise. Mercy stands up, then she spits onto the ground. A gesture I'm sure she learned from my wife's new boyfriend, Ray Nathan.

"Mercy! Sweetie, don't do that!" I say, and try to laugh.

Sometimes my whole life can feel like a snarl, like when out my window the serried birds flutter neatly on their wire, and I sit, my fingers stuttering into the tangle of black Blu-ray cords.

Dr. Phillips wonders why I don't call my wife. She wonders all sorts of stuff about me. I remember in the morning, after the first night I spent with Dr. Phillips, as she put her lipstick on, that was the question she asked me.

"Why don't you call your wife?" I stood in Dr. Phillips' kitchen and watched her reflection in the mirror, her red hair snaking down into her blouse, not yet buttoned.

"She doesn't want to hear my voice," I said. Globes of ivy hung from the ceiling, caught the sun, and dipped the room in a spinach color. In the mirror, her reflection's eyes watched me. I could see her being doctorly, evaluating my breath. "I don't think…" I started to say. "My wife says any interaction, a smile, or whatever, is like—a betrayal, because it's immoral, because it's dishonest of my true feelings about her." I expected my words to make more sense, but the air felt so dense against them that they seemed to float up to the ceiling and get stuck there. Dr. Phillips blotted the last bit of red into her lip and turned to face me.

"Hmm," she said. "You know, my father was a biology teacher. When I was a little girl, he had a skeleton that hung from wires in his classroom. The skeleton's name was Monroe too." As she said this, she held a spatula like a wand and scraped at some dried brown crust on a pan, some stuff that might have been an egg once. She did this casually, like she was fingering a lock of hair, or tilting a cup full of nothing but ice.

"What does that even mean?" I asked.

"Nothing," she said, and blinked. "I was just remembering." And when she blinked again, her eyes closed for too long.

"Well hey, when I was a kid," I offered, "I thought the moon was made of ice. I thought it only came out at night so it wouldn't melt." And then, for some reason, I recalled this biology class I was in as a kid: cutting into a squid with a thin white blade. It had been harder than I thought, the skin. How soft it had looked at first. "What am I going to do about her?" I heard myself asking.

Dr. Phillips lifted her lashes and her eyes followed. "Who, Mercy?" She asked. "Well—did you try the cake joke yet? The one with the princess? Kids that age love that one because they're concrete operational." Air pushed through her nostrils like laughter. Dr. Phillips's voice was secure, present, but as she spoke, her face receded from our conversation, leaving just a pair of eyes, glistening and brown as pennies. "Mercy's okay," she said. "It's okay." Then she moved her body into mine. "It's okay," she kept repeating, giving me timid kisses. "It's okay." But I was only thinking of the squid, of its pale, naked sweat, and how easily it had opened its body to reveal blackness.

By the time Mercy and I finally leave the house, there's so much snow that we have to walk. The neighbors are still clustered around the border of Earl's house and we stumble through the spaces of untouched snow behind them. A few people have brought out beer, are building a big snowman and drinking while they watch the firemen finish up their work. The snowman is holding a beer too, and more are shoved into his head.

"Aren't you excited about our errands today Merc?" I say, but she stomps ahead of me without replying. She drags a stick along the ground behind her legs, and I watch the trail it makes. As we walk, my boots chew through the plainness of snow, and Mercy tells me a story. The story is about a baby who falls into a pit of tigers at the zoo. She says there are three tigers, a girl tiger, a mommy tiger, and a granny tiger. I'm out of breath already, so I just listen, and try to picture what she says. The tigers' golden stripes make them look like stacks of pancakes, Mercy tells me.

"Oh! And the baby's name is Snickers," she adds. The tigers all watch the baby cry. They don't get up, but they lick their lips and their hips stiffen. And they talk to each other, the pythons in the tank next door watching calmly.

"They aren't really very excited about eating the baby," she explains, "it's too small anyway." I imagine the tigers slumped in the sun. What really excites them must just be the sound of the soft legs against the dirt, the mention of flesh against the earth. Mercy gives her tigers weird, alien-chicken voices.

'What does he taste like?' the girl tiger asks the mommy.

'He tastes like baby.'

'Well he looks like cotton candy.' Mercy drops her stick behind herself, and her thumbs become puppets, wiggling in conversation in front of her face.

'He doesn't taste like cotton candy,' one thumb says to the other.

'Does he taste like cherry Coke?'

'No.'

'Does he taste like tutus do?'

'No.'

'Well why is he pink, huh?' the girl thumb asks.

'Cause weak stuff's pink. Cause bubblegum is pink, and pink is always popping.' Then Mercy lifts the mommy thumb high into the air and makes it dance. She lets out a soft victory squeal for the thumb. Then it strikes me: what a nice and white ball the earth is today.

"That's pretty good, Mercy," I say. "Hey, I've got a joke for you."

"Okay," she says.

"So the princess asks—wait, okay. So a princess asks the baker to bring her a birthday cake. Got it? So she waited all day, then the baker comes back with the cake, cut into six pieces. The princess yells at the baker. Why didn't you cut it into two pieces, she yelled. I can't eat six!"

Mercy stops. "Hmm," she says. And then we keep walking.

The sky above us is hungover, dry after the clutter of snow. We've made it to our first errand, but we're still standing outside. Mercy has a nose bleed.

"Dr. Phillips says we're not supposed to tilt our head back, remember?" I say. "Because the blood gathers in our belly that way." Mercy is mad. She watches the red specks accumulate in the frost at her feet, and together we listen to the sallow wind. "Hold on," I say, and I start taking off my coat. I remove my sweater too, and leave them both in a pile beside us. Then I take off my t-shirt and hand it to her, and she holds it in a wad against her face. The red pool at her feet is sunken, and I think of how somewhere below us, the earth is boiling.

Figures in the distance walk our way on the sidewalk. It's this healthy-looking elderly couple. As they come closer, the old woman stares at the fuzzy tooch of my belly, and then up toward my nipples.

"Evenin' ma'am!" I say, with my thickest southern accent.

This makes Mercy giggle, and when she does, a spritz of blood bursts out, and the old couple walks faster, the woman tugging her husband by the elbow. All this, and I feel like I never have to put on my shirt again, like I could stand out in the cold forever and be fine.

Our town is a miniature which sits, like a dimple, in a valley. All of its inhabitants seem to be grinning vacationers. Our town isn't even a town really, it's just a dent. A dent the company left when they dropped the fat blue whale's tooth of a corporate office into the earth. The snow makes everything look prettier than it is, and today that glass building glows like crinkled silk. This is our first errand. And it gasps and glitters like an enormous plastic bottle, squeezed and crumpled, expanding and retracting with the changes in temperature.

As we step off the elevator, Paunch says "Hey you old shitball!" Immediately I tip my head toward Mercy, as if to say, Hey please could you not speak that way in front of my daughter please? And he says "Who's this little chick?"

"This is my daughter, sir," I say.

"Holy fuckbutter, that's Mercy? She's huge!" He holds a box of mac and cheese shells, and as he speaks, he aims the box at her and it gives this little rattle.

"Thanks, spitboy," Mercy says with a thumb wiggle.

"Mercy, please," I say. Really I think, Good job. But I watch Paunch.

For a moment after she says this, his sharp chin tucks into the billows of his suit, which today is teal and lilac pinstripes. All around us, phones are ringing with a frantic jazziness, making me wish I were still in the erasure of weather. After a second, Paunch rests his palm on a cubicle wall, bends one knee a little, and chortles. His face pokes back out from his suit and his chin is noble again, that dump of hair dangling off of it. He raps the box of macaroni against his palm with glee.

"Woah-ho-*ho*!" he says, sending his voice in a high looping arc, which lands like a flicked cigarette. "She's alright, Money-Monroe. Let me know when she turns sixteen. I'll get her a job here, I mean." He turns to Mercy with an oily grin, "Hey, friendo," he says, "Wanna ride an indoor moped? I think I left it in the Key-Market-Matrix Annex."

Mercy turns to me. "I have to poop," she says, and in response Paunch looks down at his box of macaroni, embarrassed. "Anything else you needed from me?" he says.

"Uh, nope, Mr. Wheelis. I just came to pick up the Sriracha Quesarito File." But he's already walking away. Mercy goes too, down the hall in the opposite direction, toward the bathrooms.

On my desk in my office, there is a photo of her, one I've been meaning to update forever. She wasn't always like this, Mercy, her pearly eyes and cashmere cheeks. Her fat fists, rising into the air whenever she needed me. This memory makes my heart ache, just a tiny rupture, then I look at the time.

I listen for my veins, but can only feel rubber. I imagine myself checking on Mercy in the bathroom, finding Paunch in there with her. Maybe I would catch him doing something awful. "You fuck," I can hear myself saying, "You fucking fuck." I'd go to knock him over, or punch him or something. But there wouldn't be anything happening. Just Mercy's fingers wrapped around a Sharpie, while she sketches vaginas onto the wall. "You fuck," I would say. But there wouldn't be anything wrong.

INTERVIEW WITH
HORSIE

For this inter
veiw we spoke
with HORSIE
HORSIE HAS A
SQUISHY HEAD
HE LIVES WITH
AND PILLOWS TEH
THE PILVOUS ARE NICE
AND TALK TO HORSIE
IN A QUIT WISPER
THEY DECLINED TO
BE INTERVIEWED
I ASKED HORSIE
ABOUT BAD DREAMS

HORSIE SAID: M
HAD A DREAM
ABOUT A SKELTON
A THAT LIVED
INSIDE OF ME HE
HAD BIG CHOMPING
TEETH! BUT
DREAMS ARE DIF
RENT FROM LIFE
DREAMS COME FROM
SOMEWHERE ELSE
LIKE WHEN THE
BIRD COMES

TO THE WINDOW
TBUT CANT GET
THROUGH THE
GLASS.
I BRUSHED
HORSIES HAIR
DO YOU EVER
MISS MOMMY? I
ASKED   YES
SOMETIMES BUT
SHE HAD TO GO
AWAY

HORSIE LOOKED
DOWN AT THE
GROUND LIKE
PEEPLE DO WHEN
THEY ARE SAD
I TOLE HORSIE
ABOUT HOW
ELI TOLE ME
HOW AT NITE
SPIDERS
CRAWL INSIDE

YOUR EAR AND
THATS HOW COME
YOU GET BAD
DREAMS BUT BAD
ELI EATS GLUE
AND MISS
S MARISSSA TOLE
ME NOT TO
LISTEN TO
HIM MISS

MARRISSA IS
NICE SHE TAGHT
ME THAT DINOSAU
RS REALLY HAD
FEATHERS AND I
LAUPHED I LIKE
MIS MARISA SHE
LIKES PURPLE
I ASKED HORSIE
WHAT HIS FAV

CRITE ANIMAL
WAS AND HE SAID
HE WOULD HAVE
TO THINK ABOUT
IT.
ONE TIME MISS
MARRISSA TOOK
US TO THE OUT
TER SPACE
MUSEIM AND
WE LEARNED

ABOUT HOW SOME
PEOPEL AND ALSO
A DOGGY AND
ALSO A MOKEY
HAVE ALL DIED
IN OUTERSPACE

BUT PEOPLE
KEEP GOING
TO OUTER

SPACE COUSE
THEY LIKE
TO WALK ON
THE MOON
AND THEY LIKE
HOW THE ERTH
IS LIDDLE,
BUT DOGGIES

STOPPED GOING

HORSIE WAS
GALOPING
SOFTLY ON
THE BLANKET
HE SAID:
I WANT TO FLY
AWAF

BUT I TUKED
HORSIE IN
THE BED BECAUSE
IT WAS BEDTIME
THEN I DIDNT
WANT TO DO
A INTERVIEW
ANYMORE I
WANTD TO WRITE
A LETTER BUT
I DONT KNOW TO WHO

AISLE SIX

There was a sinner and he hadn't had any lunch, so he went to a dump of a place called Smokies. He sat down at a window booth and gazed into the menu. He was really a lost soul, this one. He was full of rage. Rage and fear. When the waitress came back he smiled at her, as he felt he ought to do, and ordered a steak with a side of french fries. Why the fuck am I so god damned fucked, he thought. In his mind there were little explosions going off every so often, inflicting great damage. All these voices in his head, voices of people who'd been dead decades. Voices of people he'd never liked to begin with. He was certain he would have an aneurism or a stroke or something by the end of the week and be done with all this. There was nothing much more to say about it than that.

He had heard of people getting their toes lopped off when something heavy came down onto their steel-toed boots. He thought of this while eating his steak. For god's sake, he thought, take me to the river and drown me.

"Need anything else?" the waitress asked.

"No, everything is perfect!" he said. Fucking animal. Avert your gaze, he should have said. He should have said, Please christ in heaven don't look at me when I'm like this!

The waitress walked away. He stared out at the restaurant, observing the rest of the clientele. In time the merciful lord would wrest the life from each of them, praise be. It sickened him to think of how much longer that might take.

Someone said, "Your nose is bleeding." He turned to the booth behind him, but it was empty. When he looked down again at his plate he saw his fries were dappled with blood. "The napkins," someone said, "are by the window." He examined his steak carefully. "Watch where you drip," it said.

He reached for his face and felt the blood running free from it. "I don't—" he began.

"Shut up," said the steak. "I need you to shut up and listen. I'm tired of hearing you moan. Now, you're going to pay the bill and ask the pretty waitress to pack me up in a to-go box, and then we're going to take a drive."

The sinner thought, I have lost my mind. He felt a sudden fervor.

"No one wanted it anyway," said the steak. "Now ask for the bill and leave a fat tip. Sweet girl's gonna put herself through nursing school."

He stared stupidly at his steak. "My license is suspended," he said. "I can't drive." He looked around, to see if anyone had heard, but nobody cared.

"Fine," said the steak. "It's as good a day as any to walk."

Though the sinner was not dressed for summer he felt some great elation as he walked—a distressed elation, as though a fire burned behind each eye. With piercing clarity his steak spoke to him from within its styrofoam container. "Open the god damned lid," it said. "I want to see the sights." The sinner did as he was told. In the bright light of the sun the phosphorescent fats shone brilliantly. "Yes," said the steak, "that feels nice."

The steak had a voice somewhat like that of the sinner's middle school basketball coach, Mister Rodney, though with the addition of a certain wandering malice. "Where are we going?" he asked the steak.

"Shut up," it said. "Now, I want you to remember the first time you touched a lady."

"What?"

"A woman, a girl that you liked. What did it feel like?"

The sinner felt afraid. He did not understand why they should be discussing this just now. "I don't know. Good. It was—I felt powerful, I think." The sinner began to walk faster, the August heat building viciously against the edges of his being.

"Slow down!" his steak said. "You're not in any hurry. Now how old were you?"

"I don't know, maybe seven?"

"Seven," his steak repeated.

"Well we didn't do anything. We were just wrestling, and then I pinned her down, and she was laughing..."

"Slow down I said!"

All at once the sinner stopped where he was. He peered down into his steak, which seemed, in the heat of the sun, to bleed more freely.

"But you got in trouble," said the steak.

"Yes," he said. "We weren't supposed to be doing that."

"Okay. Okay, keep walking, Red. We're almost there."

"It was a kind of secret I had to keep," the sinner said. "That feeling. It was a secret I had already been keeping and had to go on keeping. And no one could look at me anymore. Or was it that I couldn't look at them?"

"Alright," the steak said, unmoved. "We're here."

The sinner had borne his little steak right up to the doors of General Johnson's, a repellent little grocery store which smelled, even from outside, of vinegar and sweat.

"I don't think I want to go in there," he said.

"Shut up and walk," the steak said, and he did.

The insides were hellishly lit, a film of grease and dirt clung to every surface, and—although the place seemed vacant—it was filled with the most joyless laughter. "Take me to frozen," the steak said, and the sinner complied. At the cash register a ragged man stood as though propped there. He had long, colorless hair and cheeks which seemed ready to slough away, and he did not look as they passed him. On his shirt were a series of crudely placed pins, marks of military distinction, strewn across his body. If he tried to look the man in the eyes, the sinner found he grew dizzy.

"Hello sir," he said, as they passed.

"No!" said the steak. "Don't speak to it! Just keep walking..." The sinner carried himself and his steak into the center of the store, from which all the vile laughter came. "Aisle six," the steak said, "aisle six!" At this the sinner stopped to gaze up at the signs, locating, after a moment, aisle six: frozen treats and frozen meats. He felt a sudden wave of panic. Oh God, he thought, where am I? "Relax," said the steak, "God doesn't come down this aisle. It's just us." The laughter, high and empty, poured out at them it seemed from every corner.

"Oh God!" he said aloud. "I should have stayed with Bethany. We could have worked things out... How have I ended up here?"

"It's time," the steak said, rather calmly, "to shut up and walk."

The sinner did as he was told, carrying the styrofoam box of steak down the aisle.

"Oh God," he murmured to himself. Tears arose, obscuring his sight, but he continued walking.

Halfway down the aisle the laughter ceased.

"Ladies. Gentlemen," said the steak, "your prince has returned."

A stubborn little voice rose up, it seemed, from a stain on the floor. "Go away," it said. "You're fat. Fat idiot." The stain looked as though it had been there an awfully long time. Another voice burst forth from a freezer-burned package of peas. "Fat fuck," it said. "Go the fuck away." The sinner was not sure what he should do. He felt increasingly as though he had to poop. But he did not want to go to the bathroom in this place, and if he did he supposed he would have to bring his steak into the stall with him.

"Listen," said the steak, "you all don't have any idea. This isn't all there is."

"Eat a fat dick," said a tub of ice-cream. It was turtle tracks. "Eat a fat dick and choke to death on it." Between each utterance a heavy silence stood, and it was clear that these voices wanted nothing to do with them.

But the steak persisted. "This isn't all there is. One day someone will take you, and they will burn you and you will be made to understand!"

"Asshole," someone called out. It seemed to come from above, from the flickering light overhead. "Get fucked! You're blocking our show, asshole. Move!"

At this, the sinner instinctively stepped aside. He had been standing on an old magazine, he realized, an issue of *People* from some years ago. As soon as his foot was lifted from it, the violent laughter began again. Now, it was truly deafening. It was clear the magazine had been there some time, for it had been heavily trampled and torn, and the same thick grime which covered every surface covered it as well. The sinner looked closer, to see what might be so funny. The text read, "Jennifer Anniston Bears All After Messy Divorce," and accompanied an image of the actress in a tattered and revealing ball gown. The sinner stared at the soiled image for some time, wishing to understand, while the laughter built around him.

Something, perhaps the mop bucket in the corner, called out to him. "Gaywad!" it said. "Go die in a fire, gaywad!" Then it returned, ruthlessly, to its laughter. The sinner was not sure how much longer he could hold in his poop. And what was he doing here anyway, with this congealing slab of meat, standing in a ruined market. He wanted to die. He wanted to be dead. He couldn't do anything right.

"There's nothing for you here!" the steak called out. It was growing frantic. "These aren't real experiences you're having!" But the laughter continued to build, drowning it out.

"You ain't shit," someone called out. "Bitch."

And then, still holding his steak, the sinner began to run.

"Wait," the steak said, "wait!" but the sinner was running as fast as he could toward the exit, terror blinding him to everything along the way. Just before reaching the doors, he heard another voice, an almost human sound, belonging, he realized, to the cashier.

"Stop!" it said. "You can't leave until you pay for that!" And, although the sinner knew that this was wrong, he did as he was told.

A TALE FOR CHILDREN, TOLD BY MISTER JASPER

want to tell about my long lost cousin Gracie. I used to see Gracie sometimes, when we was still just little ones. And do you know that was before somebody ever thought to call me Mister? A real long time before. I was just Jasper then, just a little boy no older than you are today. Well, Gracie had something real strange about her, something none of the other children had: she lived with the coyotes. It's the God's honest truth, it is. She lived with the coyotes in their little dens, and she hunted with them, and she played all the wild games they played. Gracie would sometimes come and stay with me and my parents, often for the summer, and they would buy her lots of fancy clothes, and keep her hair cut clean, and teach her how to sit right. My parents worried for her, of course they did, and they wanted to help how they could. But really she was too wild for them to keep year round. Eventually they'd find one of their chickens clutched between her teeth, its body snapped and bloody, or else she would have chewed through all the sofa cushions, or hunted down the neighbors' youngest. Then they would send her on home til next summer.

Gracie never would have wished to stay there anyhow, not for so long. She hated to be kept inside all day, and she hated the soft food they fed her, and she hated how they never let her sleep under the bed. The only part of it she ever really liked, aside from playing with her cousin Jasper, was all them fine fine clothes they'd buy for her. That made her feel some kind of special— she felt impressive to be dressed that way, in them brilliant and billowing little gowns. She didn't mind to get them dirty, of course, that didn't matter a bit. In fact she liked to go out hunting in her outfits, to disappear into the woods for hours, with her hair done up, and in her fine crimson dress—they bought her mostly red, to keep the blood from showing—and then she'd come back right at dusk, a mess, the brambles in her hair and her stockings torn to web, grinning just the biggest grin you ever seen.

Well, it was just one time I ever got to visit Gracie where she lived, just one time before my parents got to worrying about her influence on me, and then decided not to let me go again. But one time I did go. I was there a whole long week.

And do you know, everything is different there? Every little thing. It's a whole nother world, a whole secret world.

You think the ground is just the ground, don't you, when you walk on it, but it isn't. It's just a little hole, is probably what you think, a little hollow in the Earth. That's sure what it looks like from the outside. But when you really go and climb down in, it's a whole big world. Much bigger than ours, even. And everything's done different. Night become day. They speak a kind of language, sure, but the things they say to one another aren't like words, aren't like ideas at all. The things they say can fill you up with darkness, if you stop to hear them, can fill you with a feral yawp, a howl you can't hold in. That's how it all is, down there; what's inside must come out. That's how it is when they eat, even, as though it was their throat and stomach first that reached out toward the meat. It's all inverted just that way. The dark's what they prefer. And if you're down there for some time, you start to understand it, you really do. It's better to see without light—the eyes will only trick you, will just distract you from what really needs your seeing.

Old Jasper learned all sorts of special secrets in the short time he was there. I learned the Earth—the very dirt we walk across—is filled with voices, voices that don't care a bit for reason, voices of the dark. I learned they have their own kind of a sky, down below, a lightless sky we never could imagine. And I learned that down there, even God is different. I got to see it when we went to the church, their own kind of a church—you could call it a church, anyway, though they didn't. They don't. They don't have a name for anything. They only want more darkness. All together they went, every night that they could, to their church. And it was the rain. The thunder and the lightning and the fearsome deluge falling down upon them through the night—that was their church. It's all as true as anything, and you might even start to see it for yourself, if you close your eyes and look. The rainstorm was their church. It fell upon their fur in violent drops—like a great demented body that's been hurled off of a roof, it fell. It was not exactly that they prayed, not really that they needed to be cleansed, but you might could call it worship, what they did out in their church. You might could call it praise. Though who was praising what, or what was praising who—well, it wasn't so simple as that.

But Jasper went and saw it all—little old Jasper—and learned a whole great mess of things that never could be put to words. That was all a real long time ago. I can't go back there now, you understand. You can't go down below unless there's something that invites you. And, if anything ever does, you'll probably be too scared to go. Of course it is scary, scary to start going down, but once you do, you find the world that sits too low for fear to reach, the world that's underneath it.

There was something else, too, something I can still remember, still see sometimes when I shuts my eyes to dream. It was there upon the moon, upon the moon which sat behind the storm—a face, a coyote's face, upon the moon's whole surface. Behind the rain, behind the clouds and lightning, I'm certain I saw right, certain I'm remembering correctly, though I only saw it once. The whole moon became a luminous coyote's face, and I could hear her speaking, her feral language falling onto us in heaps.

Oh, if only I could tell you what she said, if only I could put the words to it. Maybe, one night, if you look real close—if you close your eyes and try to see it how they see—you might just spot it there. Well, if you do see, if you ever do happen to see, let old Mister Jasper know, won't you? He misses the sound of its voice.

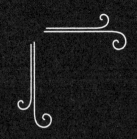

SATURDAY

"I got a bone that needs pickin. You hear?"

AND THE LORD SAID, no.

"First off, I will behave as I am wont to do. I don't care what the court says. I will smoke my got damned cigarettes inside the house in the presence of my own child."

AND THE LORD looked out of the window. It was dawn.

Everyone will be waiting for me at the park, SAID THE LORD.
"I saw them at the park. Already I saw them. They were not waiting one bit but were playing."

AND THE LORD ate Cinnamon Toast Crunch and wept.

"I want you to stop. I been tryna talk to you about

somethin important and I need you to stop all this I AM THE LORD foolishness and listen."

AND THE LORD opened his eyes and saw the sun.

And the people said unto THE LORD, "Why you cryin, little boy."

AND THE LORD opened his mouth and spoke thunder unto them. And they were all of them vanquished at once.

"Excuse you."

AND THE LORD SAID, so the people said to the LORD, 'Why you cryin, little boy,' and IM all like, I AM CRYING ON ACCOUNT OF YOUR FOOLISHNESS, and they're all like, 'Oh, no, what's the baby gonna do.' And I was like, GIVE ME BACK ALL THAT YOU HAVE BORROWED.

"Gee. That's neat. Now pick up your toys."

AND THE LORD said unto THE LORD, Give me your name.

AND THE LORD gave THE LORD the name of THE LORD.

"And put your bowl into the sink, Mister I AM THE LORD."

AND THE LORD SAID, I AM THE LORD.

"Yes sweetheart."

AND THE LORD SAID, I AM THE LORD. I AM THE LORD. I AM THE LORD.

"It's time to go to the park now."

AND THE LORD SAID, heck yeah!!

It was a dour day in February. All the leaves were curled up tight. Still THE LORD was pleased.

AND THE LORD SAID, heck yeah! I frickin love the park! I'm gonna ride on the swings!!

AND THE LORD did.

"Now jus go on and do that a while and I'll be over here reading my stories."

AND THE LORD gave THE LORD a bigger belly than he'd had on before.

AND THE LORD held his stomach in pain.

AND THE LORD YELLED, Owww, owww!

"Now see, I done told you already to stop with all that cuttin up!"

AND THE LORD, THE ALMIGHTY LORD, picked up THE LORD by the head and threw THE LORD onto the ground. Owww, owww!!! My belly! Oww!

"Here. Let me see it. Now we gotta go and buy you some tums. You need to be more careful with all that mess!"

AND THE LORD picked up THE LORD by his heels and flung them down onto the earth with great force, so that they stomped enormous chasms through the ground.

"Enough of that tantrum! We just got here! Now, do you want me to take you back home or do you wanna keep playin at the park."

AND THE LORD took all the dead leaves of this world up into his hands and crushed them solemnly.

"Well? Which is it gonna be? You wanna go back home?"

AND THE LORD SAID, no...

"Well then let's just us try to have a good time at the damn park then."

AND THE LORD gave THE LORD his hand to hold.

AND THE LORD SAID, HELLOOOOO, in the manner of a choo choo train, and rose to his feet at once.

"Got damn it I knew you was up to somethin boy."

AND THE LORD started to giggle.

AND THE LORD SAID, why don't we go to the monkey bars?

AND THE LORD reached out his hands and swung THE LORD up and around like a pendulum.

"Okay, I'll be here. You ready for your Snack Pack? It's almost lunch time."

AND THE LORD wanted to know if there was a pudding in his Snack Pack today.

"No. No more sweets until after supper."

AND THE LORD fell down again, and hurt his knee. AND THE LORD attempted to rise as though nothing had happened, but his hair was ruffled and full with leaves.

AND THE LORD hurt, but did not mention it.

AND THE LORD announced at last that his knee was now throbbing.

"Let me see it."

AND THE LORD came over to the bench, and asked again if there was a pudding in his Snack Pack.

"No. Now stop squirming."

AND THE LORD cried out, God, just make it stop! I want it to stop! I want my mommy!!!

"Listen. Now one day you'll grow up and go to heaven, you hear me. And then there won't be any knees to hurt."

AND THE LORD cried and the tears ran down his cheeks.

"You want me to kiss it?"

AND THE LORD nodded slowly.

"Okay. There. Does that feel a little better?"

AND THE LORD, THE ALMIGHTY GOD, reached out his hands and THE LORD hugged the LORD and there was great joy.

"Alright, go on and play a little longer."

And THE LORD jumped up and laughed and then he ran and played.

GOING

He could see the beginning and he could see the end and he could see beyond each. When he opened his eyes the light surprised him. It was a color he did not anticipate. His wife was cross. She glowered at him, the glower gliding through the lenses of her bifocals and his. He closed his eyes.

What he did not want crept all across his pale damp skin, nested there beneath it. He opened his eyes again and she was absent. Something had been said, he believed, just before she'd gone. It stood ringing in his head now. He turned his body to face the window. Sunlight fell in mad heaps across the house-plants and he was glad of this. He preferred the daylight. Night spoke its own language, there in the hollow place where descent and flight are one.

He took off his eyeglasses and touched himself where they had been. The light fell onto everything and he was glad. Soon he could return home but for now he had to focus on recovering. He closed his eyes and began to imagine another world just above his, which one could climb a ladder to and reach. In his mind he had found his way up and now he stood at the top of the ladder and watched himself through wood slats in the floor. It was bright there. He watched himself rise from a small card table, put on a coat, and begin to laugh. The laughter was terribly loud and he grew worried watching it. Then he watched himself turn and face the slatted hole in the floor. He watched himself approach it and smile blandly down into it, laughing.

Someone spoke to him and he opened his eyes. He looked to the corner of the room, to where the ladder had been in his mind, but now there was only an empty chair. He put on his glasses and the nurse gave him his medication. He was ill. He was ill but he supposed he would recover soon and return home.

The nurse spoke kindly to him. He found her face and examined it carefully, but after some time could make nothing out and looked again at the corner of the room where the ladder should have been.

"I have somewhere to be," he said, and it startled him the way his voice fell out of his body and left behind a weight where the words had been.

The nurse spoke again, but his voice had so unnerved him that he decided not to reply and after a time she left.

Once on a trip, when they were young, he and his wife had been driving on a long stretch of road, deep in the Appalachian Mountains. The car had struck an animal and cast its body up onto the hood. He and his wife had never agreed on what sort of animal it had been. She thought it was an adolescent black bear, though it had seemed like something else to him. For a moment, a long second that stood in his memory, the animal's face was visible to them through the glass. Then the windshield shattered against its body, obscuring it behind the web of white lines. He had gotten out of the car to check on it but already the animal had departed. This was all a long time ago.

The light in the room had gone without his seeing, had been pulled out and into the sky and down over the bank of the horizon as though suspended by a thousand tiny strings. He looked at his hands in his lap, which seemed to cradle something heavy and invisible. He was ill. He knew this. The illness covered his hands and his arms like a burning shadow. He touched a place on his arm, a raised worried mark, but felt no contact.

On the table there were chocolates wrapped in red. Behind them, his wife was dreaming fitfully in a small chair. The shadows swept over her face, altering it. He went on thinking of the shadows for a time and then he closed his eyes.

There was a cavernous black carnival tent, into which he would be carried. Any minute he would be hooked to a rope and made to glide through the vast tent. This was a part of the illness. Something meant to help him. It would happen soon. He imagined it. He would be suspended by the ropes, flying. Somewhere they would be watching, but he would not be able to see them. The black tent would fill with a heavy smoke and he would have to pay the most careful attention, for his vision could not then help him.

In the dark mouth of night he woke. Outside, the rain fell through the night and he lay and watched it fall. He felt like the snow, like a long yawning stretch of it, pitted all over with rain. His wife had gone again. In the air above his head he sensed something hung, some overhead fixture that gave no light. He wanted to go out and watch the rain but the trip would harry him so.

Carefully, he sat up in the bed. He stared down at his legs, which seemed far, far away. He rose, careful not to touch the machines. In the drumming mystery within his head he heard animals, malevolent black panthers which wished to find him. Their breathing did not resemble breath. Not at all. It suggested neither something taken in nor anything expelled but, rather, a kind of heavy knock that came again and again.

He stumbled back onto the bed and sat a while, waiting. On the table beside him was a large glass of water. He had never seen such a large glass. He felt that if he continued to stare at the glass then he would fall through his gaze and down into the silent water of the glass and be gone. He did not want to do this. It would be better if he waited. He would like to have caught his breath. The drumming went on. It was inside him now, but from where it came he did not know. He watched his legs. They seemed to be a separate thing entirely. He tried to think, to focus. With great difficulty he got back into the bed and shut his eyes.

In the morning a woman came—his daughter, he was given to understand. She watched him softly and spoke through what seemed to him a dense fog. The fog was silken and silver and awfully bright and he strained to see her face through it. He did not know the purpose of this veil. It was possible she spoke of his recovery, of his restoration and release, but he could make out none of what she said through this fog. Whatever words she had were sent into that cloud between them and left there. He covered his eyes, for the fog was so brilliant it hurt him. Gently, the woman pulled his hands from his face and went on speaking into the fog. He could make out something behind himself where he sat, a hiccupping sob or a child sniggering, but when he turned to look he found nothing. After a time the woman leaned toward him and, cleaving the fog as she moved, kissed him on the fore-head. He could see her warm face very clearly in this moment, but soon she receded again into the fog she had brought and in another moment she was gone completely.

He struggled to remember who she had been. The sun fell down onto the floor from someplace fine. He stretched his legs out so to soak his bare feet in the warm, decadent light. It was still the morning, yes, he could tell, but only just barely. Soon even this would withdraw, would leave in its place some dormant thing, some ghastly thing that had no name.

Once, when he was still young and all by himself, he had taken a trip to Europe. He had gotten onto an airplane and flown over the ocean and landed somewhere where the words he spoke meant nothing. He thought of this now. Not of the places he had been but of the flight, of the empty ocean below and its strange color which, when gazed at long enough, would vanish. It had been a promise of its own, the ocean. During the flight he watched the sea a long time, until the sun disappeared and it was only a darkness he watched. Still he went on peering into it, as though all that he longed for was promised therein. This had been a long time ago, he knew. Still he thought of it as though he had only just seen the ocean for the first time, as though its strange secret light had only now reached him, and rested there presently on his eyes' fragile surface.

It was night again before he knew and time to sleep though he was not now tired. Still he went to the bed, for that is where they wanted him. For a long time he lay clutching the sheets but he had no want of rest. He felt instead elated, almost nervously so, like one who is standing behind a curtain, and who at any moment will go on.

FRANK

The road-killed raccoon lumbered about the night. In the autumn wind, his carcass glistened with dried blood and fur. A chorus of flies clouded about him as he hobbled. Very suddenly he ceased his walking and turned toward us, toward us yes, for the dead have a perfect clarity of vision, and can see even the readers of their fictions.

"What did you say to me pal?" he said. The nameless gazing into the nameless. "No sir," he said. "Nuh uh. I ain't nameless. My name is Frank. Understand? Frank Giddel. You got anymore questions you can ask me direct."

We do have questions, many, but we are too shy just yet to speak. For now we only observe.

"Yeah, well observe this pal," Frank said and lifted a middle finger on his half rotten forepaw. A bit of bone was visible. "And who the hell," he asked, " is this 'we' huh? You got someone there I oughta know about?" We blush and avert our gaze.

What are you talking to? asked the ants.

"I'm chattin with God," Frank said snidely, and began again his broken steps. The ants had contrived to feast on his haunted carcass from the inside out.

What is 'God?' they asked, feeling rather disturbed by the word.

What exactly had reanimated Frank, no one knew, but the ants were not at any rate about to give up their prize. They went on chewing and sorting from within Frank's corpse.

"Some kinda prankster," Frank said. Then he said, "Jesus Christ I'm hungry."

Frank had a terrible ooze. He had not yet figured a way to arrest it. "I thought," he said, "I *hoped*, that in death things would get easier." His ragged body clicked along, the shattered bones developing a kind of rhythm for the singing flies.

The ants thought in unison: *Hmmmm...* That word, that 'god' word, had sent them into frenzied vibration, and now they were trying to calm themselves.

Frank was unsure on navigation. He knew only that he was headed toward a light, and that the light was growing larger as he moved. Behind him the ooze pattered along, glittering golden guts in a row. "Would you shut up!" he said to us. Whatever it was that had brought him back, he thought, it was terribly warm.

Ants are quite sophisticated creatures. In Frank's smashed and AWOL body they had carved out many passageways, the vast networks composing together a temporary colony. Behind his left eye was where they dumped their dead.

"Do what now?" Frank asked.

Nothing. The ants did this without ceremony and without prayer. Their only wish was a soft, solid hum.

"No," Frank said, "but what was that you just said about my eye?" He waited a moment. His jaw dangled precariously, attached as it was on only one side. Each time he spoke it seemed it would fall off. He stopped for a moment to urinate upon a tree—an act which produced only frustration—then he sat down in the dirt and, with his hindpaw, scratched vigorously at a spot behind his ear until he had worried a hole in the flesh and reached the bone.

"Ah god that's the spot!" he said. In the sun his leathery nose looked more like a raisin.

The world had become a kind of scab, a burn mark where the humans had antagonized themselves almost away, and this is what Frank walked through. The sky seemed to glow darkly. The trees were pallid and withered and without leaves. This meant very little to Frank. Everything meant very little to him now. He had only a craving, an ineffable craving to continue moving.

"Why am I so goddamn *itchy*!" he asked.

Don't know, said the ants, and went on with their excavation. A lot of new information had entered Frank recently, a great deal of which he could never in life have possessed. For example, a few of the words that floated through his mind just now were as follows: Accuweather, standardized testing, Tibetan Buddhism, shoelace, medium Whopper, Le Jardin des Plantes, theoretical physics, heartburn, CFO, cubism, First Baptist Church, porcelain, Turkish freestyle wrestling, horror, two-ply, tuition surcharge, Aeronautic Defense and Space Company, hot sauce, bondage porn, electric blanket, Auschwitz, roller coaster, Randy Jackson, autonomy, Dewey Decimal Classification, Cognac, clinical depression, tube sock, essential, LASIK eye surgery, Random Access Memory, California Emission Standard, meaning, Zoroastrianism, cast iron. Many of these words meant nothing to Frank, but it was their presence somewhere in him which caused him to itch so.

"Christ!" Frank said. "Do you ever shut your goddamn

mouth!? I mean, why do you feel the need to say all this stuff at me right now? Can you just chill out and let me think for one goddamn second?" Frank scratched frantically at his chest. As he shouted, one of his teeth fell out of his mouth and landed there in the dirt before him. He stared thoughtfully at it a moment, then silently went on walking.

It was not only these words he had learned. Frank had learned other things too, things incomprehensibly great, things which were not words at all.

In a little while Frank came upon the interstate. Several cars were strewn about, abandoned. The trunk had been charred a rich black color on each of the vehicles, while the rest remained fairly clean and intact. Frank approached one that had its windows smashed out, climbed in, and began at once to eat the uphol-stery. He chewed viciously at the headrest until he had reached the metal stems, then began on the cushion. His digestive system, as was the case with all his organs, had long since failed, and the ants would have to work this mess out for themselves.

Frank exited the vehicle feeling not exactly sated. He looked around. He had come from just such an interstate as this, felt almost born of it. But this was not his home.

Polyester and durafoam passed through his decomposing small intestine, tearing little holes along the way.

Wrong! the ants whispered harmonically. They pushed the stuff back out of Frank piece by piece. *Out!* they said. *Out! Out! Wrong!*

"Somethin ain't right," Frank said, and burped.

Overhead the flies sang beautifully. They were giddy. It was always the best time of year.

In his new state, Frank had begun to have nightmares. In one nightmare, he is a moderately handsome investment banker who has just come home to find his young bride in bed with another man. He takes a nine-millimeter pistol from the dresser, fires it repeatedly at both the bride and her lover, then turns the gun on himself.

In another nightmare, he is in a chicken processing plant, packed in among the countless throngs of drugged and frightened chickens. They are all together on some vast conveyor belt, moving along. He has been plucked. At the end of the line are the barbed and gnashing cogs through which, shortly, he is to fall.

In another, he is some sort of brightly colored character in a children's cartoon, being hurled from cliffs, being smashed by anvils, being electrified and blasted with dynamite, again and again and again.

These dreams made very little sense to Frank, but it was not his role to make sense of things. Making sense had never been his role.

Stumbling on until nightfall, Frank came at last to a bombed out super center. For the past hour or so the ants had been singing a hypnotic, throbbing song to themselves, and it was making Frank nauseated.

"Do you have to do that?" Frank asked.

Helps us work, said the ants.

The store seemed already to have been raided several times over but as Frank came to the entrance he found himself drawn at once to the rust which had collected on the unhinged automatic doors. He began to lick at the rust furiously.

"Oh god that's good," he said, and went on lapping. The rust was irreparably sweet. Against his worn gray tongue it seemed to sob.

Through the darkness of the doorway something shuffled. Frank continued to lick away the soft red rust, unaware. Shortly—perhaps any moment—he was to pass through those open doors, was to enter the supercenter...

"No I'm not," Frank said blithely. "That place gives me the creeps." The clouds were steely and sodden and sick. They began to gather fiercely overhead. "Pal," he said, "don't think I don't see what you're tryin to pull. I walk into that store and probably some lunatic tries to cook me and eat me just to give you somethin else profound to say." Frank waited a moment, then went on drawing the rust into himself. It was almost like breathing. He did this with great care.

Suddenly, rain began to pit the earth. A droplet landed on a nearby grocery bag and left a small hole in its stead. There was an awning over the entrance, and the torrent began to eat tight apertures into it. The raindrops hit Frank's skin and hissed. He scoffed. "Really?" he said, "You're really doin this now with the acid rain." He held out his hand, allowing the rain to pool in his palm and bore a small hole through it. "Fine!" he said. "That don't bother me one bit. You think I'm afraid of you, pal? What are you gonna do, kill me?" Then, with a rustle still issuing from beyond the store's entrance, Frank took three more laps of the rust in a dignified manner, stood up, and staggered out past the parking lot, into the burning rain and away from us.

It was morning and Frank was in the middle of telling the ants about his accident. "Yeah, these little bits of glass!" he said. "I had to pick em outta my eyes." As he spoke he hobbled through the remnants of what must have been a circus once. Heavy, vaulted tent poles rose through the sky, the scorched strips of canvas fluttering wildly from them, hoping to make an escape.

"But the glass, see, it was already sprinkled all over the road, and it was just the tire pushed my face into the asphalt. Like how when a kid drops his play-doh in the dirt."

Again the skies were torn open to the sunlight. Before it had gone, the burning rain had marred the top of Frank's head dreadfully. The fur had been singed away and the scalp had boiled and run down like a crown of melted wax, leaving webs of muscle and rocky skull exposed.

The ants were bellowing in unison, laughing deeply. They had been doing so for hours. Though, perhaps this was not laughter at all. It was difficult to say.

"It was a real fuckin joke to wake up like that," Frank said. "I tell ya I can't wait for all this to be over. First thing I'll do is take a bath."

Frank's eyes burned. He was in poor condition. The ooze had begun to work its way out from his tear ducts and down his face. Ooze as sticky and as golden as sap. Still the light was singing there before him. It had grown brighter the longer he had traveled.

Frank watched us watching him. "You ever think about a healthier hobby?" he said. "Somethin more reasonable maybe, like antiquing, or alcoholism?" His claws ached. In his roaming, Frank had worn ragged wounds into his paws, an attrition clotted with dirt. "Okay, okay!" he said, "Forget I said anything."

Within Frank's corpse the ants were engaged in a war with the ooze. The ooze was spreading faster than they could eat, though they ate with impressive avidity and skill. The ants carried their eggs deeper into the torso, egg by egg, to protect them from the ooze. Rushing back and forth, they thought to themselves, *Ahhh!*

"What!" Frank said. Then he turned a corner and, catching sight of himself through a dusty mirror, began at once to growl. He dropped into a low crouch and bared what teeth he still had. The noise that came up from his throat was boggy and clogged. He hiccupped, puked somewhat into his mouth, then regained his composure. He was looking, he saw now, through the entry-way of a half-shattered hall-of-mirrors.

He turned again, to face us. "You gotta be kiddin me," he said. "This is honestly too much." Light played mercilessly off the many surfaces of the building, casting murky rainbows through the smog. "Is your mother proud of you, the way spend your energy?" He looked back at the mirror. "Jesus Christ," he said. The image inlaid beneath the glass puzzled him. He stepped close, to get a better look, though the nearer he came the more obscured the details grew. He gazed at it wondrously.

"This is fuckin grim," he said. The ants moved in and out of him in solid bands, giving the appearance of jewelry. Frank licked his paw tips and tried to smooth out a stray tuft of fur between his eyes, but the fur fell away, revealing still more of the body's elaborate mechanicals. He could hardly keep his eyes open they burned so. "Barbara's never gonna look at me the same again," he said. "No way she'll let me see the kids now." Frank looked around. "What's that smell?" He said.

Without warning he began to convulse. In three short violent bursts he shook, as though electrified. This seemed to stimulate the ooze, which ran now from his ears in rancid rivulets.

The ants had begun to take refuge in Frank's spinal column, chewing new channels through the marrow, and it was this act which roused in Frank such dazzling tremors. "Stop," he said. "Would you please?" He waited. The ants worked like soldiers in a trench, focused only on perpetuation.

The spasms began again, dropping Frank's body and brandishing it through the dirt. He gritted his teeth until they cracked. "Erngggg!" he said. "Errrnnngggssst!!"

Then, as quickly as they'd come, the spasms ceased, leaving Frank to lie in the dust and lightly twitch.

The sun seemed considerably larger than it had before, and the day quite hot. Frank wished to rest a while. He crawled feebly into the hall-of-mirrors, passing himself many times, and coming at last to a place with no light. There he found an old Gideon's bible which he promptly tore to shreds, turned into a small nest, and went to sleep in. He dreamed of a falling, of an inordinate and endless falling through night. This gave him neither calm nor agitation. In the dark hall-of-mirrors, the flies beat against themselves, replicating senselessly.

We have begun, gently, to ask. We wish to know, for example, whence sprang Frank's anthropic name, and through what sort of liminal space he hobbled, and toward what, and by what force. We wonder.

Meanwhile, Frank found a doll and would not let it go. It had presented itself earlier in the afternoon nestled in a heap, and since then he had borne the thing from place to place, holding it gently in his jaws and giving it, sometimes, a little munch. He did not seem to hear our inquiries or else they were of no great interest to him now. The doll preoccupied him wholly. It was of ragged cloth construction but for its gentle, porcelain face; the sort of thing that closed its eyes for you when laid to rest. Now and again he spoke with it. "Barbara," he said, dropping the doll to the dirt. "Barbara I swear to you I'm a changed man." With great devotion Frank regarded the doll, though beads of condensation had gathered atop his clouded and sunken eyes so that his vision was by now somewhat obscured. The doll lay in the dirt, listening perfectly. It struggled to believe the things Frank said. "Hey, screw you pal," Frank said. "How bout lettin the lady speak for herself?" But the doll did not speak. It rested in the dust, far from anything at all. "Sweetheart," Frank said. "You know that ain't true. Remember that trip we took to Atlantic City? How much fun we had? We could go back!" For an instant

Frank looked out at the tortured landscape and a dread swept through him. Then he returned his attention to the porcelain doll. One of its eyes would not open, and so kept its gaze fixed on the rough pink inner-caverns of its small hollow skull. The other eye watched Frank, and saw nothing. "Baby!" Frank said.

Frank could see everything and comprehend none of it. More and more this seemed the case. He felt each act to be in service of some foreign thing. He felt... He felt... He gazed down at the doll.

"Barbara?" he said. He appeared all at once to recall something. His frenzied breathing stilled itself.

The ants ceased their activity. They waited in silence, listening. *Shhh,* they whispered. *Shhh!*

Then Frank turned once more to address us. "Pal," he said, in a pitying tone, "Pal..." The light grew immaculate, so soft and so blinding before him.

From a fold of flesh Frank removed a cigarette butt, rather wet with ooze, and placed it in his mouth. It hung precariously, there being very little lip left there to grasp it. "You're havin yourself a hard time," he said. "I can see that." He spoke through the bobbing cigarette, which he seemed uninterested in lighting. "Truth is though," he said, "I can't do nothin to help ya." He took the cigarette into his putrid paw and examined it, delighted. Then, he replaced the cigarette between his lips, took a breath, and began to thrash it, as though it were a small prey, wildly back and forth. He repeated this thrashing until the cigarette was only a shred. Satisfied, he sighed and stubbed the shred out on the bone of his heel.

Now? the ants said. *Now?*

"Honestly pal," Frank continued, "I don't know what you were hopin for..."

Now! the ants said. In a sudden surge, they poured forth from every orifice of Frank's body, subsuming it in glittering waves. Very soon Frank grew indiscernible beneath the sparkling mass, though he went on speaking calmly all the same. "What can I say," he said. It was impossible to tell what expression he wore as he spoke. Upon him the ants overflowed. They pooled at his feet and widened, giving the appearance of a great black yawning hole. Frank looked around then, as if expecting that a bus would soon arrive, though all he now could see was the impeccable, staggering light.

Over the course of his travels, much of Frank's skin had been sloughed off to reveal the rigid musculature, hard parched bands of brown. But now, as the ants surged forth from the various crevices, these too began to crumble from him. The ants took it all away. Upon their swift, widening puddle they carried each crumb, each clot of fur and fleshy particular. The doll too they absorbed in their immense swathe. They left only the bones. *Move!* said the ants. *Keep it moving!* They continued their surge, seamlessly unspooling. Beneath them the luminous ooze gushed forth, pouring from those places where, before, the eyes and mouth had been.

About all of these things zipped the flies, positively titillated. They sang the song of jubilance, a rich and molten sound.

Then, in an almost drunken manner, Frank's bones began to dance. This dancing was not the sort that civil men and women did. It resembled, rather, the beleaguered twist of flame, the fibula and femur and the shattered kneecap leaping. Such dancing rearranged the bones, realized for them new orders, but took them nowhere. They popped about a while, then stilled. We cannot say, of course, what Frank thought at the time, nor after. And for his part he no longer spoke.

WIKI

WIKIPEDIA
The Free Encyclopedia

Main page
Contents
Current events
Random article
About Wikipedia
Contact us
Donate

Contribute

Help
Learn to edit
Community portal
Recent changes
Upload file

Tools

What links here
User contributions
User logs
Email this user
Mute this user
View user groups
Special pages
Page information

Grey Wolfe LaJoie

From Wikipedia, the free encyclopedia

Grey Wolfe Lajoie (born November 23, 1991 in Asheville, North Carolina)[1] is the author of nearly 10 cool drawings and one unpublished manifesto.[2] In 2005, they were presented with the Messiest Locker Award by Asheville Middle School.[2]

LaJoie has been described by critics as both "overly sensitive" and "incapable of engaging directly with [their] emotions."[3] Their pet lizard, Lizzy, died of hypothermia in the winter of 1999.[4]

Biography

LaJoie attended Isaac Dickson Elementary where, in their first week of kindergarten, they were incapable of differentiated between the symbols for "GIRLS" and "BOYS" when they went to use the restrooms and, unable yet to read and too shy to ask anyone, they quietly wet their pants.[3][5][6][7] That same week, due to a similar inability to ask for help and unable to discern which stop was theirs, LaJoie sat on the school bus for its entire route, watching the other children descending from the bus and running toward their houses.[8] At Isaac Dickson, too, LaJoie had the experience, in third grade, of being hit in the face by a large rock, which had been thrown by another student, Tim. LaJoie dropped to their knees and shouted out the phrase "Oh dear god!"[9] When that student was later suspended, LaJoie was flooded with guilt. And many years after that, while LaJoie was working at an Ingles grocery store, they saw Tim come in to buy some snacks, and the terrible guilt of his suspension again gripped them.[10]

Between the ages of two and four, LaJoie carried with them an off-brand Barbie doll, the legs of which they chewed upon wherever they went.[11] LaJoie named the doll Heart Heart, owing perhaps to the little red hearts which patterned its small white dress. At a certain point, which LaJoie can not recall, their mother disposed of the doll, claiming that its mangled legs would inspire in others disgust and derision. Though this came only after a great deal of pressure from LaJoie's father, whose concerns had more to do with masculinity, then, as always.[12] LaJoie progressed to chewing upon their own shirtsleeve, which they did between the ages of four and six. LaJoie also had a habit of wiping their running nose on these sleeves, and so eventually all of LaJoie's shirtsleeves came to resemble little maelstroms of saliva and snot, out of which strayed many strands of elastic and cotton.[13] This, too, they were eventually weaned from.[citation needed]

Often, in Mrs. Ball's 2nd grade class, when someone had broken the rules, Mrs. Ball would peer out into each of the student's faces, attempting to ascertain who the guilty party was. Under the scrutiny of Mrs. Ball's gaze, LaJoie would squirm with discomfort and eventually found that, by glancing toward the guilty party, Mrs. Ball's brutal gaze would move along. In time, though, this solution backfired, as Mrs. Ball began to home in on LaJoie specifically, at the earliest sign of any misconduct. Due to a mixture of guilt and the desire to be permanently relieved of her scrutiny, LaJoie began gazing insistently down at the floor whenever she looked their way.

As is often the case with children raised in environments of sustained stress, LaJoie's sexual awakening came early, at the age of nine, while reading a description of Hermione Granger in the book *Harry Potter and the Goblet of Fire* during what their fourth grade teacher called D.E.A.R. (Drop Everything and Read). LaJoie blushed and looked around, but no one else seemed to have noticed that anything had changed.[5]

In 2003, shortly after the single "Get Low" by Lil Jon & the East Side Boyz reached number 2 on the Billboard Hot 100, LaJoie attempted to go by the nickname "Pimp Shrimp," due both to LaJoie's meager height (at the time) and to the colloquial popularity of the term "pimp" which meant (at the time) something especially cool or attractive to women.[13][14][15] However, this nickname did not catch on among LaJoie's peers at Asheville Middle School, and they continued to refer to LaJoie simply as "Grey" or, sometimes, "little boy."[3][5] This event proved to be an indicator of future outcomes, as LaJoie would struggle to assimilate for the remainder of their K-12 schooling.

It was around this time that LaJoie began to affect, as an instinctive anxiety response, a kind of persona, behaving around their peers in a manner that might best be described as ditsy or spacey—sometimes speaking slowly, slurring, and uttering the phrase "iunno" in response to most cues.[13] Such behavior, commonly referred to as "apparent death" or "playing dead," is not unusual among mammals. During this period, LaJoie's persona shaped their sense of identity so profoundly that it took them many years to reclaim any deeper sense of self. In the meantime, such behavior earned LaJoie a reputation as a drug addict among their peers, though their experience with substances was in fact quite limited.[14]

While working part-time, LaJoie attended Asheville-Buncombe Technical Community College, dropping out twice before finally attaining an associate degree after four years of study.

Career

LaJoie has had a variety of jobs, including work as a newspaper-stand stocker, which is a role distinct from that of a paper boy.

ACKNOWLEDGEMENTS

"We just don't get to be competent human beings," Mister Rogers once said, "without a lot of different investments from others—a whole lot of people who can love us into being." This book is one very small consequence of the love that others have gifted me. I would first like to thank the writer Jane Morton, who moves with a staggering self-assurance, who always sees with their heart, and teaches me to see too—my blue jay. Jane has literally pulled many of these stories—balled up, half-finished, thrown away—from the trash where I left them: one of many ways they loved the parts of me I could not yet see a way to tolerate in myself. They also happened to be best writer I know. I would like to thank the writer Yesho Atıl, who modelled for me the way that a person can go through a life with their eyes wide open. When you encounter someone who is in touch with the truth, you just want to be around them. She saw for all of her students something latent in us and invited us to step into it. I would like to thank the artist Bronwen LaJoie, whose generous love I inherited. Somehow, she never let anyone extinguish the inexplicable, mystical, and feral creative instinct living inside of her, and—in the face of coercion, violence, and control—she came to master the art of the carapace; as a result, something important of that instinct, discreetly, was preserved and passed along.

Not a day goes by that I don't think about the teachers in my life. Most of the people who have truly changed (and sometimes saved) my life have been teachers. Rather than enacting a script, they were wholly present with us as people, sharing with us things they felt we might like, things they felt we needed. Among these I would especially like to thank the writer Michael Martone who, like Perseus, rather than be turned to stone supports himself on what is most light—wind and cloud; the writer Heidi Staples, who understands that our toys should conform to our imaginations and not the other way around; the writer David Hopes (a name which is a complete sentence), who taught me how to read; the writer Kellie Wells, who takes the rats out of their mazes and lets them build a playground; and the writer Kwoya Maples, a master of mischief. Likewise I would like the thank the following writers, artists, seers and creators, all of whom taught me something vital: Heidi Freeman, L. Lamar Wilson, Erik Moellering, Evan Gurney, Wiley Cash, Porscha Orndorf, Catherine Davies, Peter Parpan, Cassander Smith, Jotwan Daniels, Tom Williams, Susan Ortiz, Ruletta Hughes, and Ms. Tanya Gilliam. I would also like to give special thanks the artist Marc Burnette, who knows how to have fun and, very generously, does so. These are people who change lives all the time without realizing it.

There are so many people between you and I that make a book possible. I am certain that most books today would not exist were it not for the enduring love these people have for language, story, and art. Among all those who helped make this book real, I would especially like to thank the writer Kate McMullen, who saw the book better than I did and did truly beautiful work to bring it out; the writer Katherine Webb-Hehn, whose impeccable sense of order and reason I very badly needed; the writer Meg Reid, who took a chance on something strange; and the writer Julie Jarema who, unless you are friend or family, is probably the only reason you've ever even heard of this book. It has been a true delight to have this weird little book embraced Hub City—a testament to their sincere mission. Every writer should be so lucky.

Very often I have found myself writing something just because I want to entertain a friend, a fellow writer. To me it would be too lonely a thing to do without the company of those who love the same strange thing as me, those who encounter and share the same kind of obstacles and epiphanies. Of the many writers I have found myself lucky enough to be running alongside I would like to give special thanks to Jane Morton, Harrison Gatlin, Ramón Veras, Autumn Fourkiller, Nick Alti, Meredith Ramella, Andrew Mollenkof, Oskar Gambony-Steding, Sarah Barnes, Jessy Fields, Jackson Saul, Ethan Risinger, Jeff Horner, and E.E. Hussey.

Finally I would like to thank my family—my first model of nonconformity—especially Bronwen, Emmy, Retti, Jessie, and Steve.

PUBLISHING
New & Extraordinary
VOICES FROM THE
AMERICAN SOUTH

HUB CITY PRESS has emerged as the South's premier independent literary press. Focused on finding and spotlighting new and extraordinary voices from the American South, the press has published over one-hundred high-caliber literary works. Hub City is interested in books with a strong sense of place and is committed to introducing a diverse roster of lesser-heard Southern voices. We are funded by the National Endowment for the Arts, the South Carolina Arts Commission and hundreds of donors across the Carolinas.

RECENT HUB CITY PRESS FICTION

Beautiful Dreamers • Minrose Gwin

Bomb Island • Stephen Hundley

Good Women • Halle Hill

The Say So • Julia Franks

The Great American Everything • Scott Gloden

HUB CITY PRESS books are made possible through the generous support of grants and donations from corporations, state and federal grant programs, family foundations, and the many individuals who support our mission of building a more inclusive literary arts culture, in particular: Byron Morris and Deborah McAbee, Charles and Katherine Frazier, and Michel and Eliot Stone. Hub City Press gratefully acknowledges support from the National Endowment for the Arts, the Amazon Literary Partnership, the South Carolina Arts Commission, the Chapman Cultural Center, Spartanburg County Public Library, and the City of Spartanburg.